PRAISE FOR EVANGELINE WALTON

For *She Walks in Darkness*

"Driven by unceasing suspense and intriguing historical mysteries, this Gothic adventure simply won't let you stop reading it."
—Tim Powers, author of *The Bible Repairman and Other Stories*

"For those of us who loved Evangeline Walton's lyrical and energetic quartet retelling the Four Branches of The Mabinogion, *She Walks in Darkness* is a startling but quite gripping change. It begins with a mystery, shifts quickly into horror with Gothic overtones as the narrator fears for her life in an ancient, rambling villa built above a labyrinth of catacombs, then it reveals its background of romance, and resolves into a fast-paced art history thriller. The tale, set in a sere and lonely region of Italy, combines Walton's detailed knowledge of art, mythology, and archeology. Her wonderful descriptions bring life to the underground paintings, statues, and bones that have been buried in the tombs and haunt the living as they stumble through buried history with flashlights and illuminate, one flash at a time, the immortal faces of myth. *She Walks in Darkness* is a remarkable gift from the past."
—Patricia A. McKillip, author of *Wonders of the Invisible World*

For the Mabinogion Tetralogy

"Based on the mediev   series ranks with the best of

ekly

"[Walton] has achieved her own beautifully idiosyncratic blend of humor and heroism."

—Ursula K. Le Guin

"Walton updates these ancient texts in a very 20th-century manner, without losing their sense of magic and otherworldliness."

—*SF Site*, featured review

"Is Walton's the Mabinogion [Tetralogy] worthy of being called a 'Fantasy Masterwork'? In my opinion, yes."
—*SFF Masterworks Reading Project*

For *Above Ker-Is and Other Stories*

"Most of Walton's short stories are, like her novels, seamless blends of history, myth, and local color.... Walton tantalizes the reader with the possibility that seemingly supernatural events have a perfectly logical explanation."

—*Locus*

"The book is a delightful collection of charming, stylish fiction probing the darker side of the human condition. Not to be missed."

—*SFRevu*

"...well worth reading, and re-reading."

—*Mythprint*

SHE WALKS
in
DARKNESS

EVANGELINE WALTON

TACHYON
SAN FRANCISCO

Tachyon Publications
1459 18th Street #139
San Francisco, CA 94107
(415) 285-5615
tachyon@tachyonpublications.com

smart science fiction & fantasy
www.tachyonpublications.com

Series Editor: Jacob Weisman
Project Editor: Jill Roberts

ISBN 13: 978-1-61696-133-6

Printed in the United States of America by Worzalla

First Edition: 2013

9 8 7 6 5 4 3 2 1

BOOKS BY EVANGELINE WALTON

The Mabinogion Tetralogy

The Virgin and the Swine (1936)
[retitled *The Island of the Mighty* (1970)]
The Children of Llyr (1971)
The Song of Rhiannon (1972)
Prince of Annwn (1974)

Other Novels

Witch House (1945)
The Cross and the Sword (1956)
The Sword Is Forged (1983)

Above Ker-Is and Other Stories (2012) [fantasy short stories]
The Swan-Wife (2013) [verse drama]

For further information
please visit evangelinewalton.com

TREASURES FROM ANTIQUITY

PAUL DI FILIPPO

R eader, you hold in your hands something I myself
have always longed for but never thought
possible: heretofore unseen fiction from Evangeline
Walton. In addition to a new book of her short stories—
Above Ker-Is and Other Stories—and the reprinting
by the prestigious Overlook Press of her entire
Mabinogion quartet, *She Walks in Darkness* seems to
point toward a new phase of Walton's posthumous
career, where she can finally receive some of her long-
overdue accolades.

As a fan who has been enjoying her books for more
than four decades, since Walton was revived in the
Ballantine Adult Fantasy series of the early 1970s—
the late-career break that introduced her to so many
readers—I positively rejoice. This upsurge in her
posthumous career is invigorating not only to Walton's

literary reputation—which unfortunately has rested immovable on a too-low plateau for an inordinate number of years—but also to my deep pleasure and yours as well.

Walton's early life (she was born in 1907 and died in 1996, a good long span that happily allowed her to savor her own literary revival) strikes me as archetypical in its lineaments of lonely, sensitive, literate, home-schooled child (supported by an appreciative mother) who falls naturally into a writer's life. One might almost cast her as the protagonist of the recent novel by Jo Walton (marvelous synchronicity of surnames), *Among Others*, which charts just such a biography.

After completing a goodly number of trunk projects, Walton scored her first publication at the tender age of twenty-nine. *The Virgin and the Swine* appeared in 1936 and would later form the springboard for the second stage of her career, when it was reprinted by Ballantine as *The Island of the Mighty*.

Now at this point in history, female fantasists who could serve as role models and networking colleagues for the young Walton constituted a rare species indeed. Hope Mirrlees had given the world her *Lud-in-the-Mist* in 1926. E. Nesbit, of course, remained inspirational, but for "children's books" only. In the pulps, C. L. Moore, partially invisible as female behind that initial-heavy byline, had appeared with "Shambleau" in 1933. And on various tables of contents, circa 1936 and prior, were to be discerned

Clare Winger Harris, Leslie F. Stone, Francis Stevens, Lilith Lorraine, and a host of others, their pioneering efforts most notably charted in Justine Larbalestier's great study of the era, *The Battle of the Sexes in Science Fiction.*

So at this point in the realm of might-have-been, Walton's career could have received a lift and guidance from genre solidarity. But such a fate was not to be. Her dismal, go-it-alone track record with lame and unhelpful publishers had begun. Also, her chosen lifestyle—rather in the pattern of such other apron-string homebody authors as Robert E. Howard, Flannery O'Connor, and Eudora Welty—did not conduce toward collegiality.

Walton's next big break came in 1945, when August Derleth printed her novel *Witch House* as part of the Arkham House catalogue. No one could have provided better entrée into the whole genre ecosystem than Derleth, whose roots extended everywhere. But for whatever reason, Walton was not instantly swept up by genre readers and writers. The female solidarity she might have availed herself of then could have come from such luminaries as Andre Norton and Leigh Brackett. But fate dictated otherwise.

Walton kept writing, but it would be another ten years until her next book appeared, *The Cross and the Sword* in 1956, and then another long slog until the Ballantine rediscovery began in 1970. So slight was Walton's footprint on the field that publisher Betty

Ballantine and her editorial consultant, Lin Carter, both thought *The Virgin and the Swine* had fallen into the public domain, its author deceased. Upon learning otherwise, they eagerly relaunched Walton's career.

But previous novels consigned to her trunk remained unknown and unappreciated to the present, despite the Ballantine revival. The one we are lucky enough to hold in our hands now, *She Walks in Darkness*, constitutes one such (with others soon to follow its delayed entrance into print). It was apparently written in the early 1960s, marketed briefly, and then shelved.

Once again, had Walton developed any connections, she would have been supported, I am sure, by the largest clade of fully professional female genre writers yet extant: Kit Reed, Margaret St. Clair, Mildred Clingerman, Marion Zimmer Bradley, Katherine MacLean, Zenna Henderson, Sonya Dorman, Rosel George Brown, Joan Hunter Holly, C. C. MacApp, Andre Norton, Evelyn E. Smith. Bradley, who went on to write Gothics (the mode Walton employs here) might have been particularly helpful.

Certainly Walton would not have needed any assist from her peers on the actual writing. *She Walks in Darkness* is an utterly deft and competent production—no castoff, disposable item, but rather a thrilling blend of gothic and mystery, like Daphne du Maurier meets Cornell Woolrich. (We can imagine Walton's counterfactual career as having a second track to it, akin to the CV of Patricia Highsmith.) Add in a soupçon of Thomas Burnett Swann's fascination with the eerie lost ambiance of the classical Mediterranean, and you have a very enjoyable read. I will try to convey something of its ambiance without spoiling its plot.

The tale is narrated by Barbara Keyes, young and newly married to Richard Keyes, an archaeologist working in Italy. The American couple is planning to base themselves at the Villa Carenni, outside Volterra. But upon their arrival, Richard and Barbara are beset by dastardly villainy. Add in the fact that the Villa Carenni is built atop ancient Etruscan ruins, including a lost temple dedicated to Mania, Queen of the Dead, and you're almost in A. Merritt territory.

She Walks in Darkness is very much a product of its time. Barbara's voice is that of the devoted housewife who's just recently been tipped to the existence of Betty Friedan and is now considering the merits of Ms. Friedan's thesis. Bright, lively, smart, Barbara is nonetheless a bit timid, prone to succumbing to male dominance. As for knowing her own libido—well, let's just say she knows it better after this little adventure, especially the time spent in the arms of handsome local lad Floriano, who manifests at the Villa at a crucial moment and proves central to the mystery. Still, despite some dithering and indecision, Barbara does take vigorous action at several crucial moments and lifts off the page in breathing verisimilitude. Her husband's loving appreciation of her solidifies our own estimation of her worth. And Walton captures her voice unerringly. The first-person narration is always assured in its telling, even when Barbara teeters on the edge of panic. Given the nascent second-wave feminism of the early 1960s, with all its uncertain feints and pulse-takings and embryonic dialogues, Walton and Barbara stand out as on-the-tip harbingers of something big just down the pike.

The novel gets a bit expository at times, but such passages always constitute important and interesting backstory vividly recounted. The reader will greedily ingest engaging material about the Etruscans that will surely propel collateral investigations. And when the mood shifts to action sequences, they zip suspensefully along. No one can fault the long perfect set piece where Barbara is led to an obscene revelation in a manner that is positively Lovecraftian. In fact, at times this book reads like the best Roger Corman film never realized, with all these named actors used in their primes: Vincent Price as Count Carenni, Jack Nicholson as Floriano, John Agar as Richard Keyes, and Barbara Steele as Barbara. I can almost see this movie flickering on my parents' B&W Sylvania set right now.

Players at the game of literary history enjoy indulging in counterfactual exercises, such as my speculations about how Evangeline Walton might have had a different, more successful, lucrative, and acclaimed career. But in the end, we are left with what actually happened. And in Walton's case, the reality isn't so bad after all: honest work appearing at longish intervals, followed by a second efflorescence and a posthumous band of dedicated readers—Walton herself does not have to walk alone in the darkness ever again.

CHAPTER I

Old Mattia Rossi's body is gone. It no longer lies at the foot of the cellar stairs. This morning, when I finally braced myself to go down and look for those keys I need so badly, it was not there.

And that can mean only one thing.

He is not in hiding. He did not rouse and crawl away into the dark, as a crushed worm might crawl. He does not lie suffering somewhere in those black, net-like passages. To search for him there would drive me mad, I think, though I suppose decency would drive me to it. But he cannot be suffering; he is dead.

Yet he is gone.

I know what other people would say, if they were here to say it. "He never was there. You had a nightmare. You never would have dared to go down into those cellars by yourself."

But I did go down, and he was there. If you could call that flat, bloody thing himself.... That queer flatness, a kind of emptiness, was what told me he was dead. It was worse, somehow, than the crushed part of his head, than the stains.... It is gone now, that thing that used to be a person. A person I never met, but whom people I know knew and liked. Someone must have taken it away. Who? Who—except the murderer?

That means that he did not go away after he killed old Mattia. Or that if he did, he came back.

Is he here now? Lurking somewhere in this huge place? Watching for me, perhaps, with those eyes I never saw and must not try to imagine. Listening....

I must get help! Yet how can I go away and leave Richard alone here, hurt? My husband is unconscious; no sane man would hurt him. But if the murderer thought him only asleep—

It would take me hours to walk back to Volterra, even if I did not get lost. And there were a great many turns in that long, lonely road, that very lonely road.... The village would be nearer, but even if I could find it, I can speak only five or six words of Italian. How long would it take to make someone understand me, help me?

Perhaps the murderer does not know that we are here. He need not know. There are so many rooms in this old Tuscan villa. All the rooms above ground—two stories of them. All those dark chambers and corridors beneath the real cellar, God knows how many of them, leading God knows how far down into the bowels of the Earth! Those old Etruscan tombs that Richard was going to study. Not Christian catacombs, such as underlie old houses in the Campagna, but a veritable city of the tombs of men who died before Christ was born, before Rome became an empire. So many dead— and only one live person can be anywhere near us! But it is the living who are terrible....

Perhaps he will stay down there, the murderer, in that everlasting darkness where he belongs. Maybe he is looking for treasure, of which those old Etruscans had so much, and will find it and go away. But last night he did come upstairs. Or someone did....

I can't leave you, Richard! I can't!

This time yesterday we were on our way here. Side by side in the car, sometimes laughing and talking, sometimes just sitting there with the sun in our faces, and the mountains jutting into the blue sky above us.

"They used to be volcanoes," Richard said once.

I said, "I hope they're extinct!"

"As craters on the moon," he answered comfortably. "There's still fire underground. Enough to keep up those giant pillars of steam at Larderello, and to make the earth smoke in some places. But no more fireworks."

"Well, I hope we can depend on that. This country makes you know what 'scorched earth' really means. It looks burnt—burnt from inside."

It did. We had left the pleasant Florentine country-side behind us, with its villas and vineyards, its gracious ordered beauty. Sometimes we still passed olive groves, their trees like fountains of silvery-green spray. But those bright spots were growing scarcer: There were more and more long stretches of pale, barren clay. The mountains looked stark and harsh and forbidding, lifeless as mountains on the moon. The earth itself had a queer, whitish look like seared flesh.

It wasn't exactly my idea of honeymoon country, but I didn't mean to let Richard see that. He was so proud because Professor Harris, a man famous in the field in which Richard still considers himself a beginner (I think several well-qualified people already consider him more than that), had asked him to take over his work at the Villa Carenni that summer, work begun five years ago, just after World War II ended. Professor and Mrs. Harris are on their way home to America now, on a long-postponed vacation.

"You'll find the villa pretty isolated. Not a neighbor within miles." Mrs. Harris had warned me about that. In that Florentine hotel to which I had come to marry Richard, she had given me a good deal of advice. "It's a beautiful old place, though. The kitchen is antiquated—I did all our cooking on two electric hot plates in a kind of gorgeous medieval powder room. But you needn't worry about having to carry your garbage downstairs; old Mattia will always do that. He came with the place; I think he was born on it."

But Mattia Rossi never will carry anything anywhere for me....

Yet then, safe in that Florentine hotel, with people all around us, how could I have dreamed of anything like this? And if I had had any inkling of danger, I should have expected Richard to be here with me, quiet and strong. One can't imagine anything melodramatic happening anywhere around Richard. But now he lies in the next room, sleeping that strange, death-like sleep from which I cannot wake him, and the car lies outside, a mass of charred upholstery and seared metal. The car too....

We are trapped. And we rode into that trap so happily, expecting to find a place where we could laugh and love!

By noon yesterday we had stopped laughing. The heat of this arid land had baked all humor out of us. We were glad when the car finally came within sight of Volterra, D'Annunzio's famous "City of Silence," that old Etruscan city whose power and splendor the Roman butcher Sulla wrecked. Its tremendous walls still stand, the walls that even Sulla could not storm; he had to starve out the city. We drove into it through the Porta all' Arco, that true Etruscan gateway deep as a small house—it is over twenty-five feet thick. Three giant stone heads crown the cyclopean archway, midnight-black against its yellowish-white stone. Time has eaten up their faces, but they still seemed to stare down at us, full of a quiet, terrible power.

"Who are they?" I asked. Somehow it seemed natural to say "are," not "were."

Richard shrugged. "Gods, probably. Nobody really knows."

"Just what does anybody really know about your precious Etruscans, Rick?"

"Not too much. They called themselves Rasenna. The Romans believed they came from Asia, and a few modern crackpots make their starting point Atlantis. Certainly by the beginning of our era they were being called 'a very ancient people, like no other in their language and customs.' I'd say their tastes were rather birdlike. They ate insects dissolved in honey, and did everything to music—from kneading the dough for their bread to flogging their slaves."

I winced. "I wonder if the slaves appreciated their masters' aesthetic tastes."

He made a face. "I doubt it. But Prince Mino Carenni might have approved. He was very proud of his Etruscan descent, and anything but democratic."

"The late owner of the villa? He doesn't sound like a very pleasant person."

"Prince Mino lived in the past, and feudal power wasn't too far behind him. Sometime in the 1860s, his grandfather is supposed to have had a disobedient servant executed."

"You don't mean it!"

"I do. And Prince Mino believed in the good old days. He got into trouble when the war ended; he was lucky to get off with being put in a sanitarium. He may still be there."

"He'd been one of Mussolini's men, then?"

"Lord, no!" Richard chuckled. "Imperial Rome herself was an upstart in his eyes, let alone a butcher's son. Though he might have deigned to advise Mussolini if properly asked. Rome had had Etruscan teaching and some Etruscan blood, so a revival of her glories would have been better than a world dominated by crude Teutonic barbarians like us. Nazis, English, Americans, we were all just one step above animals."

"When the Germans entered Italy, he certainly must have been annoyed."

"He was so incensed that he never again set foot outside the villa. Until the war was over."

"Then how did he get into trouble?"

Richard was silent a moment, then said reluctantly, "There was some story about an escaped prisoner of war. He was traced to the neighborhood of the villa. The Germans searched it, but couldn't find him. Later a servant of the prince's went to the Allied Occupation authorities and accused his master of murder. The Allies seem to have thought there was something in it."

"But why on Earth would he do such a thing?"

"According to the informer, the two men quarreled. The escaped prisoner was an archaeologist too. A young Englishman named Roger Carstairs."

"So the prince might have taken him in?"

"For awhile they may even have worked together. The prince apparently was concealing what he considered important discoveries from everybody, especially the Germans. Most people still believe the informer's story—that the two men fell out over buried treasure. There's been plenty of that found in the tombs; Etruscan goldsmiths had their secrets—they did work that nobody could match again until this last century, with its scientific discoveries. But from what I've heard, neither man would have cared for gold."

"Then what was the trouble about?"

"God knows. Prince Mino was a great scholar, but a little mad. The Carenni family was just a little too old, I think.... Here's the Palazzo Verocchio now. We'll see if Dr. Pulcinelli's at home."

We drew up before what looked like a small fort: a massive old house of the grayish native stone. Dr. Pulcinelli, who lives there, is another lover of the old Etruscans; Richard had promised to look him up.

He was at home, and welcomed us warmly: a distinguished-looking, gray-haired man who still would have been remarkably handsome if he had weighed thirty pounds less. His English was excellent, in a bookish way: generally very formal and rather flowery.

He greeted Richard enthusiastically. "So you have come, my young friend. And with a bride as beautiful as her for whom the villa was built!"

I said in surprise, "I didn't know the villa was built for a bride. Why didn't you tell me, Richard?"

Richard looked uncomfortable. I saw Dr. Pulcinelli shoot him a quick glance, but his shrug was casual. Artistically so.

"Your pardon, signora. I should have said remodeled. Nobody knows when the villa was first built. But in the sixteenth century, it was greatly altered and made beautiful for a young lady who herself must have been very beautiful indeed. For though she was but a poor shopkeeper's daughter, Prince Carenni married her."

"Are you sure it wasn't the prince who was poor? And the shopkeeper who was rich?"

He smiled at me. "You think, like all Anglo-Saxon young ladies, of your Signor Browning's masterpiece. Of Count Guido and that most poor little Pompilia. But no, signora, this prince had both great wealth and great pride, and his little principessa brought him no fortune but her face. He spent a king's ransom on this love nest, as you would say it"—clearly he was proud of knowing this Americanism—"to make all things lovely for her, that young bride of his old age. Hers is the house you will see."

The villa's bridal beginnings didn't sound so romantic to me, after all. To think of a young girl shut up in a lonely country house with an old man made me shiver. But I thought it politer not to say so.

We had a very English-style tea, then I left the two men alone to talk antiquities while I went out to buy groceries. I had no idea what to expect at the Villa Carenni, and this might save a trip later. The doctor kindly sent his housekeeper with me as guide.

"Giovanna knows all the best shops, signora. You will need her help."

Giovanna also knew no English, and I wondered just how we would manage, but somehow we did. She was a stout friendly woman, with soft black eyes and a voice as soft, and she did know where to find the best fruits and vegetables, and also several more fattening things. I have no doubt that her cooking was responsible for both her figure and the doctor's.

Yet it was while I was with her, in those narrow old streets, that the first hint of trouble came. Although it may have had nothing to do with what happened here, I do not know that it did.

Once Volterra was a mighty fortress, the westernmost outpost of that culture that may have been brought by hard-eyed, black-bearded princes from the East. The land was fertile then, before pagan Rome crushed her great rivals and teachers, the proud Rasenna, whose own empire once had stretched from sea to sea. The Romans, later such great builders themselves, let the wonderful Etruscan irrigation system fail and the rich farmlands become deserts and ague-ridden marshes.

"Maybe, so long as Tuscan lands were rich, even Rome was afraid," Dr. Pulcinelli had said at tea.

Certainly the disasters never have been repaired. The city's prosperity never has come back; its broken walls hold only a third as many people as they housed in the days of their strength. Over them loom two buildings modern by comparison, one the famous Mastio, in whose terrible circular cells many a state prisoner of the

Middle Ages died. It holds common criminals now, and in the huge bare lunatic asylum of today it has a gloomy twin. Sight of that grim pair made me shudder; I always have hated the sight of prisons; I would much prefer dying to being shut up and knowing that I never could get out again.

"Fuggito! fuggito!" It seemed only natural when I heard a woman cry that, saw her running across the gray stones. She stopped and talked with Giovanna; their eyes flashed, and their hands and tongues flew. I gathered that a prisoner had escaped, and told myself that I must not be glad. It might be someone dangerous.

But when the other woman had gone and Giovanna led me down a steep alley filled with whitish dust, I suddenly knew that I was not glad. The massive stone walls presented an unbroken front with no corners for an escaped convict or lunatic to dart around, but I found myself watching the heavy shut doors uneasily. What if one of them were to burst open?

What if he were to jump out at us?

Shrewd criminals do not risk unnecessary bloodshed, but madmen kill without reason....

Then before one door I saw something that made me stop, startled. There, beneath the burning summer sun, was what looked like a snowdrift: a gleaming, piled-up whiteness.

Giovanna stopped too, knocked. An old woman opened the door, her wrinkled face tense, her black eyes gleaming with fear. "She's heard of the escaped prisoner too," I thought, with a pang of pity. But at sight of us she relaxed, greeted Giovanna volubly, and stepped back to let us in.

The place was the shop of an alabaster carver. Alabaster abounds around Volterra, and the old man who came forward to meet us had carved it into dozens of exquisite shapes. The white gypsum dust piled outside must have been his leavings. I do not know much about art, but I know that he is an artist.

There was a flood of Italian—I caught the words "Villa Carenni" and figured that our address was being given—but fortunately or unfortunately, the old man knew some English. Richard and I are not rich, we are saving for things our house will really need when we get it, but I finally let him sell me an exquisite lantern (a copy of an old Etruscan lamp, he said) at a price that seemed absurdly low.

His eyes beamed then; he thanked me in voluble Italian. As the money changed hands, I heard a faint rustling somewhere in the gloomy depths of the shop behind us, and the shopkeeper started and glanced over his shoulder.

"Is somebody there?" My eyes followed his, but the shadows were too deep; I could see nothing.

Then the old woman laughed—a little too loudly— and her husband moved rather quickly to the door, bowed, smiled, and opened it. They did not seem afraid that anybody might have gotten into their house; if anything, they were anxious to get us out of it. Once, on our way back to the palazzo, I glanced back, thinking that I heard steps on the stones behind us, but I saw no one.

When I joined Richard and the doctor, my fit of nerves was over. I forgot to mention the escaped prisoner, I was so busy showing my lantern, and hoping that Richard would like it. He did. Dr. Pulcinelli smiled indulgently.

"I should have known that Giovanna would take you to the Credis'; Taddeo Credi's wife is an old friend of hers. But you were not cheated; he is a fine workman. He was once a protégé of Prince Mino Carenni, on whose lands he was born."

"You knew Prince Mino?" I asked.

He hesitated a moment. "In my youth I revered him. His learning, not his opinions and theories, which were always extreme. I still admire that."

"You and Professor Harris both made a thorough search for those epoch-making discoveries that he was rumored to have found during his last years," said Richard. "Didn't you, sir?"

The doctor sighed. "Yes. But we found nothing. And we went deep into the vaults below the villa, into the lowest"—he hesitated again—"at least the lowest known level of the ancient tombs."

What a place to have built a love nest, I thought— *over a cemetery.* What I said aloud was something quite different: "You don't think that the prince would have committed murder?" And then I could have bitten my tongue; since the two men had known each other, such a remark was intolerably tactless.

The doctor stiffened. "That story was a lie, signora: a stupid and malicious slander." He paused a moment. "Yet there may have been reasons for its telling. This is a day of change. Too much change, however it ends, to please older men like me. Old loyalties are fading, old resentments sometimes erupt in barbaric ways. Not too far from here last year, an ironmaster was burned alive in his own furnace, by men some of whom he had known all his life."

"Communist agitators prompt those things, though, don't they?" Richard said. "Men from outside?"

"Communists, yes." The doctor's face was grim. "But such men are not always strangers; sometimes they return to their own birthplaces to bring violence and bloodshed. But to return to our subject: The Prince Carenni's pride of race and birth amounted almost to insanity, but it is preposterous to suggest that he ever would have harmed a guest whom his house sheltered. There is a famous old Italian story of a father who killed his own son for betraying a guest to the law. Even though, according to one version, the fugitive was also the seducer of the boy's sister."

Richard nodded. "I know, sir. You see, Barby, the guest's own worth didn't matter; the host's honor was at stake, once he'd given him shelter. In Italy the tradition of hospitality always has been very sacred."

"Exactly." Our host was gratified.

He courteously urged us to stay for dinner. "Then you could see *le Balze* in the dusk. The site of Volterra's great landslide. The event itself was a catastrophe, destroying perhaps priceless tombs, but at twilight, when the broken cliffs gleam with phosphorescence and the masses of fallen earth turn purple—well, it is not a sight to forget."

I felt that I could stand the deprivation; also that in a country so full of tombs, the destruction of one batch could not have been too great a loss. Richard must have read my feelings in my face; he thanked the doctor, but refused.

"My wife is tired, and we want to get to the villa before dark; I don't know these roads too well. But we'll be back. May we take a rain check on your invitation, sir?"

And then the meaning of rain check had to be explained; the doctor was delighted with the new phrase.

When we came to the Porta all' Arco again, a policeman stopped us and I tensed, but after a swift exchange in Italian, Richard grinned at me. "It's all right, Barbs. We're not being arrested. They're just stopping all cars to look for a man—"

"I know. I heard while I was out with Giovanna."

If I hadn't stopped him then, Richard might have told me what now I would give so much to know! As it was, he only shrugged. "Whoever the fellow is, they've certainly got the wind up. This man even wanted to look in the trunk of our car, but I told him it hadn't been unlocked since we left Florence."

It had been. I had unlocked it before I realized that the groceries could be stuffed into the back part with our luggage. The car is—was—new, and that lock sticks; I don't use it if I can help it. Did I get it locked again? I know I tried to—I am sure I thought I had. But I was nervous then; until Giovanna and I were safely inside the palazzo's stout walls, I couldn't shake off that creepy feeling that we were being followed. And if the lock didn't catch, the trunk sat there accessible for nearly an hour. Someone could have gotten into it easily; the street is lonely and quiet there outside Dr. Pulcinelli's door. Someone could have lain hidden there while Richard and I drove out of Volterra. Death doubled up in that cramped space, coiled there like a snake. Waiting to strike.

When Richard parked the car and came into the villa with me, it—that thing we had harbored—could have crawled out.

Death free to strike!

But if so, where was Mattia Rossi then? He should have been there to welcome us, and he was not. His killer must have reached the villa before us; I only hope that he has enough sense to be already well on his way elsewhere. Somewhere as far from the scene of his crime as he can get.

No, no murderer came with us to the Villa Carenni: That thought is mad, a fear-spawned fantasy of the night. It cannot matter now, the thing I kept Richard from telling me. Yet it could matter very much, here in this lonely place, whether that man escaped from the Mastio or from that other grim pile that houses the insane.

Madness. It is such a familiar word, yet what is a madman really like? I have never seen one, I have never known anybody who has. Dear God, keep it that way! Let me never see the thing that may have been coiled within a few feet of me, all that long way from Volterra!

CHAPTER II

Yesterday, when Volterra's brooding height first fell behind us, something made me say, "What became of her, Richard? Of that little bride who sounds so much like Browning's Pompilia? Did she outlive the old man and get to marry somebody her own age? I hope so."

He said rather slowly, "There's no record of her anywhere. All the other Carenni wives rest honorably beside their noble lords, either here or in Florence. But she seems to have vanished without a trace."

"Perhaps she eloped." I felt cheered.

He grinned. "You take the marriage vows seriously, Barby-girl. I'll have to keep an eye on you."

"You're keeping something from me now. If there hadn't been something you didn't want me to hear, you'd have told me about her in the first place. There is a story, isn't there? An ugly one?"

He took one hand from the wheel a moment,

covered mine with it. "Let's let it alone, Barbs. Every old house has seen both ugliness and beauty. You can't keep either one out."

"All right. I won't ask any more questions until we leave. I certainly will then."

"Good girl." He squeezed my hand, and we drove on.

Sunset found us still driving. The hills were purple now; the earth was as gray as a dead face. There were no more houses, not a single sign of life anywhere. The car was climbing steadily, up rocky, barren slopes.

And then we saw it: rosy in the red light, its stone walls—stone that light-catching, ever-changing color peculiar to Tuscany—rising up before us with an almost tender softness of hue and purity of line. It looked so beautiful that my heart rose; I pressed Richard's hand. "It *is* lovely. The right place for a honeymoon." And he smiled at me, his eyes warm. Oh, Richard! Richard!

We drove into a stone-paved courtyard and parked before huge, heavily carved doors. Richard got out and went in to look for Mattia Rossi. I was left alone in the courtyard; at least I thought I was alone....

I heard nothing; I can swear to that. Nothing but the cooing of pigeons, the soft natural sounds of a summer evening, no least noise from inside the trunk. If he was there, he waited very quietly. But of course he was not there.

When Richard came back, he was puzzled, frowning. "The old fellow doesn't seem to be anywhere around.

But he can't be far away. Nothing's locked up. Better come in."

The big, shadowy hall was lovely too, with its noble stone staircase. But it was nothing compared to our own quarters, waiting above. A wide archway joined two big, low rooms that seemed magical in the twilight. On the rear wall of the inner chamber, Venus was rising naked from the sea. Nymphs were raising worshipful arms to hail her, birds were flying low in marveling delight, fish rose staring from the deep. In the half-light the blue waves really had the shimmer of mysterious depths; their cool hues brought out the rosy whiteness of the goddess's flesh. As we crossed the anteroom towards the magnificent carved bed at her feet, we seemed to be caught among all these creatures swarming along the walls to do her homage.

"Some bridal suite," said Richard, grinning.

For a moment I didn't answer. Realization had come like a blow, made me a little sick. These had been the long-dead little principessa's rooms! I suddenly wished that Richard and I were going to love somewhere else, in some cheap, clean place. Then I managed to smile and said quite truthfully, "You can't just say that this is beautiful. But what else is there to say?"

"I'm glad you like it." Was his smile indulgent? Richard is hard to fool. "I'll go down and get our bags."

"And the groceries. I'll come too."

We made three trips in all. The first was fun, an occasion. The second definitely was not fun, and the third left me panting, anxious only to put my load down and rest.

But inspection of my very original kitchen soon restored me. It was really a bath—a Roman-ish super-bath, opening into both rooms. Walls and ceiling, gorgeous as the bedroom's own, made it a kind of rainbow wonderland. A tall screen hid the john, Mrs. Harris's two hot plates sat on a small folding table that could be easily cleared away, and the big, modern white refrigerator almost justified itself. It towered over a rose-colored marble pool that looked like the very heart of a rose. *Had the aged bridegroom like to watch his young wife bathe?* I wondered, suddenly feeling a little nauseated. *To gloat over that girlish body that was legally his?*

Richard said, "I'd better put the car away."

"Is there a garage?"

"In the base of the tower; I expect it used to hold donkeys. As we came in, a kind of screening wall hid it from the *cortile*—courtyard to you."

"Oh, the tower! I didn't get a good look at it. Can we see it from the bedroom windows?"

"A little."

Most old Tuscan villas have towers, relics of the days when every country house was both farm and fort. I ran to the windows and looked out, then caught my breath.

The tower was squat, unimpressive. It had not been remodeled for the bride, but the garden below us had. Statues gleamed ghost-pale among a glowing riot of roses and jasmine. One was a gigantic, white-winged woman carrying in her arms a life-sized youth of red terra cotta.

I said, startled, "What's that?"

"The goddess Eos carrying off Kephalos?" Richard's eyes had followed mine.

"What for? To eat him?"

"Lord, no! She was in love with him."

"Well, I'd certainly hate for her to love me!"

This was not Homer's rosy-fingered Eos; I remembered the story now. All the tender radiance of the Greek dawn-goddess was gone. This giantess's mouth, bent to her unwilling prey's, seemed more likely to bite than to kiss. One felt immense appetite, savage strength, but no tenderness. Her very whiteness made her seem like death, seizing upon warm human life.

"She's gone native." Richard surveyed her quizzically. "Etruscan ideas very likely went back to the old Triple Goddess, the Killer-Mother: Queen of the Underworld as well as of Heaven and Earth."

"Whatever the lady is, I could do without her."

"Oh, Kephalos got home eventually." Richard raised an eyebrow. "To find that his pretty young wife hadn't been exactly inconsolable during his absence."

"I'm sure she can't have thought it was any use to wait."

Richard laughed and went out. I went back to our bathroom-kitchenette and began putting things away, but first I put on a pot of coffee. The long fierce heat of the day was gone. Now that night was near, a dank chill seemed to be rising from the thick, old stone walls, in spite of all the gaily painted figures that ran riot over them. I found cups and saucers, and began to set a little table.

And then I heard it. The crash outside!

I seemed to be crawling though I was running, ages seemed to pass before I was downstairs and outside in the cool evening. Before I found that screening wall Richard had spoken of and ran round it.

The car lay overturned in a little ditch that ran along one side of the tower. And Richard lay inside it, his crumpled body somehow looking different, horribly different from the way it does when he is asleep.

I tried to get the car door open, but I couldn't. I don't know much about cars, but this one, being a Volkswagen, had its engine in the rear, so fire ought to start in the back seat. But would it stay there more than a minute? I was wearing a blouse and skirt. I tore off the skirt, stamped it down into the inch or two of water in the ditch, then, using the muddy mass of it as a shield, I scrambled in over the car door.

Richard was heavy—how could a long, lean man be so heavy? For hideous seconds I thought I could not budge him, but finally I got him halfway across the car door. Then, as I pulled and tugged at his inert weight, my heart feeling as if it would burst, the thing I feared came. The smell of smoke, the crackle of flames. I must get Richard out—I must! With all my weight, I strained against his. The muddy skirt still shielded us, but through it I could feel the hissing heat; at any second the soaked cloth must burst into flame. Tug—pull—tug. My heart was hurting as if Eos were squeezing it between her giant fingers. Trying to squeeze the life out of me, the mortal wife who was fighting her for Kephalos. I could see her hungry eyes, feel the power of her outspread wings....

Then Richard woke up. He opened his eyes and coughed.

Together we squirmed over the car door. We fell into the ditch, but that was good. The mud put out the fires that were starting in his clothing, and what was left of mine. The whole ghastly struggle can have lasted only for seconds, but it had felt like years.

Richard seemed dazed. I led him back to the villa. Twice he stumbled on the stairs, and once he stopped and rubbed his hand against the back of his head; it came away bloody. When we reached our room, he sat down heavily on the bed, and I ran for the coffee, but he would not take it. "Let me be, Barb. I'm sleepy."

For a moment I don't think I breathed at all. Somewhere I have heard or read that it is a very bad sign when a person whose head has been hurt says, "I am sleepy."

I caught at him. "Richard!"

"Let me be." He mumbled the words that time; then he pulled away from me and just lay down and went to sleep.

My first panicky impulse was to shake him awake; fear of hurting him stopped me. Then I remembered: the telephone! The Harrises had said they had one. It wasn't up here, so probably it was downstairs in the great, shadowy hall. I made for the stairs again, staggering as I ran, my breath coming in ragged gasps.

The telephone is there, but it will not ring.

When I finally accepted its silence, I sat down and cried. But then a comforting thought came: This explained Mattia Rossi's absence. He had gone into town to report that the telephone was out of order. He would soon be back.

But he was an old man, and Mrs. Harris had said that he used a cycle. What if he should spend the night in Volterra?

Again I fought panic, tried to remember more things that Mrs. Harris had said. There is a village somewhere among the hills, not too far from the villa, but when I had asked her if anyone there might speak English, she had laughed. "Child, the people live practically the same way their ancestors did thousands of years ago. You couldn't make a soul understand you."

A village I couldn't possibly find in the dark, and where nobody would know what I was saying if I got there! An old man who might not come back till morning! I began to cry again.

Stop it, Barbara! Get a hold of yourself. You can't afford to go to pieces now.

Something deep inside me said that, and I knew

it was right. I went back upstairs; the coffee was still fairly hot, and I drank it all, black. While cold water poured into the tub, I tore off my ruined blouse and undies (trousseau things that I had been proud of), then plunged into that rose-colored marble pool. The non-voluptuous, stinging coldness shocked me back to life. Then I did what I could for Richard; I could not turn him over or get all his clothes off, but I carefully examined all of him that I could see. There is an ugly wound on the back of his head, but the bone around it feels firm. His skull is not fractured; I am sure of that. If only I knew enough to be sure!

Concussion. That can keep a man unconscious for hours, perhaps days. Even a doctor can only let the patient lie still and rest. Usually the man wakes of himself; often concussion is not dangerous, I believe. But sometimes it kills.

Oh, Richard! Richard!

Well, I had done all I could. His other hurts seem to be only bruises and minor burns, and I washed them with soap and water. I longed to drop my aching, still filthy body (I had not stopped to scrub the mud off) down beside him, to sleep and forget. But something made me stagger back into the anteroom and bolt the heavy door, the only door that connects our quarters with the rest of the house. I don't know why I did that. Perhaps it was pure childish fear of all those vacant, darkening rooms around us, of the black maze that surrounded us like a twilight jungle.

At any rate I did bolt the door, and now I thank God that I did.

I dropped beside Richard, too tired to draw the curtains. The garden was a pit of darkness now, but the white giantess, Eos, towered above it like the very Angel of Death. The fading flame of the clouds behind her gave her a look of wrath, of outraged power. As if she had just been cheated of her prey. The red light soon faded. But as I watched her huge wings darken, I was reminded of a giant bat's.

I turned my head away; I didn't want to see her. That is the last thing I remember....

Sounds woke me; I sat up sharply. Moonlight filled both rooms now, strong enough to show everything but color. Richard was breathing regularly, normally, beside me. My hand groped for him, and for a second the feel of him reassured me.

Then they came again—the sounds at the door!

The great, carved slab of wood was stirring, ever so slightly, in its ancient place. Its hinges creaked.

Somebody was trying to get in!

Not knocking—at a knock I would have jumped up, joyfully sure that Mattia Rossi had come at last. This quiet tugging at the door was stealthy, sinister. It kept on, soft, patient, determined. Whoever was out there in the hall did not want to be heard, but he wanted to get in. Badly.

I lay rigid, telling myself, *It must be Mattia Rossi. He doesn't knock because he's afraid of waking us. He's seen the wreck; he knows we've had a bad time. He just wants to be sure we're all right.*

I tried to call out, but I was afraid.

At last they stopped, those quietly horrible little noises. I heard receding footsteps, soft, yet very clear on the stone flagging.

Silence flowed back, engulfed us like gently lapping water. I rose and ran for the bathroom; it was dark in there, so I tried to turn on the light.

It would not turn on.

Neither would the lights in the bedroom, nor in the anteroom. The trunk—the fugitive—that must have been when I first thought of them. Or had their images been tugging softly at the door of my mind all along, just as that unseen but very real hand had just tugged at the wooden door?

But electricity couldn't be depended on in an isolated place like this. And there were matches in one of our suitcases. I found them, and lit the lantern I had bought in Volterra. Warm light sprang up, banishing the eerie moon-paleness, and I felt like an idiot. Of course it had been Mattia Rossi at the door. What if he had acted a little queerly: He might have had a few drinks with friends in town. I had missed the chance to get help, and now I would have to go after it. Down these dark halls, by myself. Well, it served me right.

I set my teeth and opened the door. The darkness outside seemed ready to spring at me, like a live thing, and I jerked back, then set my teeth a little harder.

No more foolishness, Barbara. You're not a little girl now, to be afraid of the dark.

I stepped out into it, holding the lantern high. My light had shrunk suddenly, seemed pitifully inadequate against all that blackness.

There was a door on my left, between me and the stairs. If it should open—

A dozen times I saw that door move. Yet when I came abreast of it, my body scraping the opposite wall, it was still shut; it had never stirred. Now was its time, though. If it suddenly should open, if somebody should spring out—

I was past it. Nothing had happened. But it still could open softly, stealthily behind me....

I went down the beautiful stairway, through the great hall, hesitated, then turned right. I had not seen this part of the house at all. Would this once have been called a drawing room? No, this next one was even finer, with white marble nymphs upholding the fireplace, the whole thing exquisite enough to be a flower.

Room after lovely room, all of them silent. Doors, and more doors, sometimes on both sides of me—and all of them like hands that at any moment might shoot out from the walls to seize me. I was a chicken, and they were all hawks, waiting to pounce—

I went right, then left. I found a room that must be the dining room, and then the huge, dreary old kitchen that Mrs. Harris had called antiquated. Doors again, more doors. I opened one and jumped back, shuddering at the Stygian darkness below. The cellars! I shut that door fast. I opened another, saw more stairs, small, shabby but leading upward. My heart leapt. This must be the way to the servants' quarters!

But it was not Mattia Rossi I met at the head of those stairs.

The man was kneeling in the darkness just beyond the top step. I saw his hard red face in the lantern light, and I tried to scream. But I could not scream, I couldn't move. I just stood there, too paralyzed even to drop the lantern.

But he did not move either, his hard red face did not change. His eyes—there was something wrong with them. And then I put my lantern down and clapped both hands over my mouth to keep back the crazy laughter. For he was an urn! A squat funeral urn, its two handles quaintly, grotesquely, like arms akimbo. The redness of the terra cotta head, the dead man's portrait, had fooled me. He was incredibly lifelike, yet death had diminished him. He sat there like some pot-bellied dwarf, staring blindly and haughtily into eternity. *Did your slaves scream in time to the music to which you had them flogged?* I wondered as I passed him.

I am glad now that I didn't laugh at him. Laughter makes a noise....

I found several cell-like little rooms, but only one looked lived in. It was very clean, as were the neatly arranged clothes and poor possessions stored in it: a man's room.

"Mattia Rossi!" I almost called his name aloud. Again, I am glad I didn't.

But where was he? Could he have gone down into the cellars for something? Had I the courage to look for him there? I must have—the sooner Richard had a doctor, the better.

Somehow I got back to that dreaded door, steeled my heart, and reopened it. I swung the lantern as far forward as I could, hardly daring to hope its light would reach the bottom of the stairs. But it did. I saw him.

Blood stained his gray hair and the gray stones around him. He lay very still; he had that queerly flat, empty look. Yet my first thought was only that he had fallen, hurt himself. I ran down to help him. But when I saw the bloody wreckage of his head, the wide, glazed eyes, I knew. This wasn't Mattia Rossi. Not any more. This was no accident either, but the brutal work of human hands.

I ran back upstairs. I left the door swinging wide behind me. Did that open door mean something to whoever came later? Did he remember that when he left old Mattia, he had closed it? Can human flesh and blood be callous enough to be sure about a thing like that? After such an act as his?

If he is, he knows that his handiwork has been seen. Dear God, let him be sane enough to be afraid—to run away!

CHAPTER III

I never dreamed that I would be able to sleep again that night, but I did. I woke with the mid-morning sun in my eyes, with Richard breathing quietly beside me. For an instant I was happy; then everything came back.

But Richard was breathing; he *is* breathing! Everything could be so much worse, so much, much worse!

I got up, wanting coffee badly, but there was still no electricity. I had to eat cold bread and butter and fruit, but they were wonderfully good. I didn't realize, until I tasted them, that I had had no solid food since I left Volterra. It brought my strength back, and I sat down and tried to think things over.

Perhaps it is not the prisoner from Volterra. Probably no escaped maniac or professional criminal hid in our car and came here with us. I wish that that illogical fantasy would stop haunting me! But somebody may have heard of all those fabulous discoveries that Prince

Mino probably never made, have come here to look for gold. Only scholars understand that all buried treasure is not gold....

I can hear Richard's voice, saying, only a few days ago, "The Rasenna had great goldsmiths, Barby. I've seen a queen's jewels—necklaces, brooches, breastplate even, a mass of pure gold—and yet all of it put together didn't weigh more than a bouquet of roses. There's no telling what treasures this country still holds. For ages Etruscan tombs have been looted, yet there's still plenty to be found.

"It's an off chance, but old Harris just might find something big. Bigger than anything that ever has been found. Prince Mino believed that the villa had been built over the site of an ancient temple to Mania, Queen of the Underworld."

"Mania?" I remember being surprised. "I didn't know that that was ever anybody's name."

"It was the old Etruscan name for the Queen of the Underworld before they began using Greek script and names, and identified her with Persephone. Her rites weren't pretty. Roman records mention the substitution of poppyheads for the kind of offerings she'd received earlier."

"The heads of prisoners of war? Was she something like an Aztec goddess?"

He made a face. "Little boys' heads, honey."

"Richard!"

"You needn't look like that, Barbs. Every holiday

weekend at home we probably sacrifice more kids to our fast driving than poor old Mania ever got in a month of Sundays."

"That's different. Nobody who's driving a car intends to kill anybody; they just do it. And people who get run over don't know it's coming. They don't have to wait—expecting it—"

"They die all the same. Painful, bloody deaths. Not always as swift as those on an altar."

"It's horrible, Rick, but it *is* different."

"That's a woman's argument for you."

"I am a woman, Richard."

His eyes kindled. "I know. My woman. Come over here and stop talking."

We were so happy, there in Florence! If only we had stayed there....

Later that same day, I remember asking, "What made the prince think the Queen of the Dead had had a temple there?"

"His ancestor built the villa over the site of an old monastery. One deserted before the ninth century, probably because of plague. Prince Mino had a coffer full of fragments of the old monastic records; they've disappeared, along with most of his own notes, but one passage is known to have read something like this: '... that demon-mistress of the damned to whose nefarious and bloody worship this place was dedicated of old... the wrath of that power of Evil still pursues us whose holy house was built here to wipe out the memory of her abominations.' And then just a few broken words: '...Mania...mistress here through the ages...Pilgrims....'"

"And that's all?"

"All his highness ever showed anybody. But he hinted that he'd found much more. That the temple still existed down beneath the tombs and that it held copies of the famous, long-lost Etruscan books. Even of archives brought by Tyrrhenus and Tarchon—the mythical migrating princes from the East. From their original 'High Place,' their fabulous lost city of Tyrrha, from which our word 'tower' comes. Records written in gold in a lost script as well as in a lost tongue, not the modified Greek alphabet that the historic Etruscans used."

"And you think it could be true?"

He chuckled. "Old Harris and I would gladly settle for a lot less. That pre-Greek script's probably bosh, but the lost *Etruscan Discipline*, as it was called—the books containing their history and the Divine Revelation that gave them the laws they lived by"—he sobered, his eyes shone—"That was real, Barby, And it would be the biggest find since Knossos!"

Also in an underground temple there could be many other marvelous things. Statues, vases, the offerings of generations of pilgrims, some of them, perhaps, of pure gold....

So many people will do anything for gold. Many who would not rob the living will rob the long-dead. Somebody could have come here intending to do only that, and then have panicked when he ran into poor old Mattia Rossi. A person who killed in panic would surely be horrified when he saw what he had done, would surely run away as fast as he could.

But somebody did try our door last night! What if it is a madman? If he is still here? Waiting, watching....

Stop that, Barbara! Or you'll go mad yourself.

If only I could talk to you, Richard! If only you would open your eyes and look at me, with all the warmth and strength and steadiness that are you! But you only lie there like an image, an empty, three-dimensional image of yourself. Where are people, when they are asleep or unconscious? Can one really snap into and out of being like that?

I am alone, and I must face things by myself. Either the murderer has run away, or he is still here. In this house, with us....

I can do one of two things. I can go for help, or I can stay here, behind this barred door, until help comes.

But when will that be? Did old Mattia have any regular visitors? Richard and I know nobody in Italy but Dr. Pulcinelli, and he has already received us, entertained us. Now he will wait for an invitation from us. No milkman will come, no postman, as they would at home. All that old Mattia could not raise on the place, he bought in town, and we were to pick up our mail in Volterra.

And Richard needs a doctor!

I must go for help. Down that long, lonely road that

even yesterday, from the car, looked so godforsaken and forbidding.

Perhaps with someone following me? Someone who can't afford to let me get help?

No! No! I can't do that! I will stay here!

But the heaviest door can be battered down. No vines or trees are dangerously near our windows, but Mattia may have had a ladder. There are tools, too, that can take the hinges off the strongest door. And nobody to hear me if I scream.

The murderer could come at any moment. Even now.

I must go, I must! And leave Richard alone behind an unlocked door? I can't do that! I can't!

But Richard needs a doctor.

For a little while I cried. The sound was terrible; I began to seem to hear it from a distance, as if someone else were making it. But it was one terror over which I had control; realization of that helped me. I stopped.

There must be keys somewhere. Probably in Mattia Rossi's room. Keys would give Richard some measure of safety....

I opened the door. Stepping out into the corridor was like jumping into a deep pit, but somehow I did it.

That other closed door again, still like a hand that might suddenly reach out and grab me. And then the stairs....

Just think of each step as you take it. Not of all the many more that you must take.

In the kitchen, in front of that open door that showed

the cellar stairs, I stopped for a second, frozen. They looked so dark even now, at noon. As my grandmother's back stairs used to look in Indiana, when I was very small. I could almost hear my dead mother's voice again. "There's nothing there, Babsie. Nothing at all."

But this time there is something there, Mother. A murdered man, and maybe his murderer. I may be near you....

I went on, trying not to imagine soft footsteps padding up those stairs, then coming up behind me....

I climbed that little third stairway, I passed that dreadful little man who is a funeral jar—a Canopic jar, I think Richard would call him. He was still smirking, just as he may have smirked, ages ago, at pleading slaves who didn't want to be flogged, even to music.

Mania, Eos, whatever your name is, have mercy on us who are beneath your outspread wings!

I made it. I reached Mattia's room, ran frantically into it. Behind its bolted door I ransacked every drawer in it, and found no keys. Then I ran back downstairs and ransacked every drawer in the kitchen too.

There are no keys!

Has somebody taken them? Nobody who was leaving the house would have....

Like a trapped animal, my mind tried to scramble away from that thought. Could Mattia have taken the keys with him when he went down into the cellar? I hadn't seen them, but then I hadn't really seen anything last night but his poor old body and the blood around it.

Could I make myself go down there to look for them?

I had to; I couldn't leave Richard alone behind an unlocked door.

I must go down and search Mattia's body....

But he was not there. There was nothing there. No blood, no body, nothing at all.

I stared and stared. As if by staring I could make the horror rematerialize, lie there on those gray stones, and so prove to myself that I wasn't mad. Then I ran.

"What shall I do? What shall I do?" I heard myself sobbing that and, foolishly, pressed my hands against my mouth again to stop the sound. As if someone else were making it.

If I were heard—!

The great hall at last, the great stairs. The way back up to Richard! I stopped, gasping. I had to have a second to get my breath before I tackled those last stairs. No matter who or what was behind me.

I heard it then. Like an answer to prayer. Something falling—not hard—on the stones of the courtyard outside. Outside! Somebody had come!

I ran to the big entrance doors and flung them wide. I saw a bicycle out there, in the safe warm sunshine, and a young man bending over it. For a few seconds then everything was vague, but I know I screamed at him. I know I heard running feet upon the stones, and ran to meet them, my arms outstretched. Felt arms close round me. Strong arms—blessedly warm and strong!

"*Aita! Aita!*" I kept sobbing that one word against his shoulder, against the hard, wonderfully alive flesh that I could feel through the rough tweed coat. He spoke to me in Italian, but I only kept on sobbing, "*Aita!* (Help!)" I couldn't remember any other Italian word. And then what seemed like another miracle happened.

"You wish help, signorina?" He spoke in perfect English; his deep young voice was courteous, almost tender.

I said, "Oh, thank God!"

There is a fountain in the courtyard; he made me sit down on a stone bench, and went to get water. With his wet handkerchief, he bathed my face, smiling. His own face was as beautiful as any sculpture or painting I had seen since I came to Italy, and it was not carved or painted—it was warm, human flesh.

Richard is long and lean, his gray eyes are frank and friendly in his brown, pleasant face, everything about him is dear and exactly right because it is Richard, but I never have thought him beautiful. I never had thought "beautiful" a word people used of manly men. But there was nothing womanish about this young Italian; he was glowingly, vibrantly masculine, all man. I stared at him in sheer delighted wonder; such splendid life made terror and death seem unreal, far away.

Yet I said, "Be careful. There's a murderer in the house. He may be watching us."

He looked startled. "Nothing quite so bad as that, I hope, signorina."

I tried to speak calmly, clearly. "There was an accident yesterday. My husband was hurt; he's inside too, unconscious. But later I found old Mattia Rossi—the caretaker here—dead in the cellar. That wasn't an accident; it was murder."

"Old Mattia dead?" He looked startled again, even dismayed. "That is bad. But nobody would have murdered him. Nobody on Earth could wish him dead. That too must have been accident—those cellar stairs are steep—"

"It wasn't an accident! If you'd seen him—seen the way his face was hurt—" I stopped shuddering. "But I can't show you; the body disappeared."

"So?" His smile was back, gently mocking. "He cannot be dead then, signora. Doubtless he was not so badly hurt after all, and has gone for help. Once again, as so often, the telephone does not work, I take it? Or you and your injured husband would not still be here."

"No! He was dead—he couldn't have been alive!" My voice broke; I knew that he thought I was sounding exactly like a hysterical woman.

"Then how did he rise and go away, signora? He who is not your Christian Christ?" The mocking smile was as gentle as ever, with that special type of gentleness that you cannot quite tell from tenderness.

There was no use arguing; I saw that. I didn't know much about foreigners yet. For all his charm and obvious culture, he might be the type of man who has a very low opinion of women's intelligence. God knows we still have enough of that kind in the United States, though they are seldom so charming and gallant about it.

I said quietly, "He couldn't have gotten far. If you had seen his head, you'd know that. It wasn't just blood—his skull was damaged. I would have sworn he was dead. If you're his friend, you ought to be worried about him."

For a moment he was silent. My head still was not working very well, but I began to think of the things he had said. They made a kind of pattern.

"You do know him, don't you? And you were coming here. To see him?"

"I know Mattia well. I am of Volterra; Prince Mino used to send him with messages to my family when I was small. But it is your husband I was coming to see, signora—if, as I would judge, he is the American signor who for this summer is replacing Professor Harris. I write and speak English well, and of archaeology I know a little. I hoped to do typing and other work for him, as I have done them for Professor Harris."

I said, "Yes. My husband is Richard Keyes."

"And fortunate in his beautiful lady." He bowed. "I rejoice to meet you, Signora Keyes. I am Floriano Silveri. Perhaps you have heard the professor or Signora Harris speak of me."

I hadn't, and I was rather surprised that Mrs. Harris hadn't spoken of him. It would have been natural to laugh and tell me about such a beautiful young man, perhaps to warn me against spending too much time with him while Richard was at work. Richard too should have been interested in this possible helper, but perhaps he had thought he could not afford him. He and Professor Harris had talked together a good deal, but I had taken no part in their discussions of their work.

But none of that mattered now. I said, "My husband must have a doctor. He's been unconscious for hours. And even if you're right about Mattia Rossi, he must need help now too. Please—please—get back to Volterra as fast as you can!"

For a moment he said nothing, obviously thinking. Then: "First I must understand the situation a little better, signora; I will be questioned. Let me see your husband. I know a little of wounds—I might be able to give some help before I go. And this accident of his— how was it?"

I could have screamed. I wanted him to go—go. To know that help was on the way. But what he said sounded reasonable. Again, there was no use arguing.

On our way upstairs, I told him about the accident, and he looked rather surprised and made what sounded like quite sincere compliments on my courage. I was startled. After all those hours of harrowing fear, the idea of any connection between courage and myself seemed laughable.

He helped me to lift and turn Richard as I had not been able to do alone. Quickly, deftly, he examined that grim head wound that it had frightened me to touch. Once or twice the sight made me flinch. He was not brutal, but he was certainly too sure of himself to be squeamish. He said finally, "Concussion—I think that you are right, signora. None of the great bones are broken, certainly, but his unconsciousness is deep. He feels nothing. To that I can swear."

"But we can't be sure his skull isn't fractured. Please go for a doctor now. At once. And for the police."

He hesitated. "Should I not first go down into the cellars, signora? If old Mattia has crawled away into them hurt, perhaps delirious, he may, as you yourself have said, need help. Most badly."

I was terrified. "No, no—don't go down there! You might meet the murderer."

"Must we go into all that again, signora?" He was gently reproving.

Somehow I managed to pull myself together, to achieve some dignity. Or what I hoped was dignity. "I'm sorry. Mattia doesn't need help—not any more. He's dead. I never doubted that, but when I saw you thought I was only a hysterical woman, I thought it might be easier to humor you. But I can't let you go down there and face death yourself without warning you."

For a moment he seemed surprised, then, oddly, pleased. He took my hand and kissed it. "For your care of me, I thank you, signora. It is long since a beautiful woman has been concerned for me. But I have no fear."

"But my husband—it could mean his life as well as yours. And you could be hours searching in those cellars, if nothing else happened. Please, please go!" My voice shook.

I told him then of what had happened in the night. Of that stealthy, persistent trying of the door, and of how there had been no knocking, no voice. I expected him to laugh and tell me I had been dreaming, but instead he looked grave at last.

"Old Mattia would have both knocked and spoken. Someone else is here. Or was. And you cannot stay alone with that person, signora. I cannot leave you."

"You must. There's nothing else to do. I'll bolt the door—I'll be all right. And we can't be sure about Richard; waiting might kill him—"

His brows knitted. Again, he seemed to be thinking. Then he said, still gravely, *"Bene,* signora. I go. I will wait only to hear you bolt that door behind me. Let nothing make you open it until you hear my voice again. I will make my bicycle fly as a bird flies."

Now that he was actually going, I wanted to throw my arms around his neck and beg him to stay. I didn't; I smiled and gave him my hand. He went and kissed it again, courtly as any old Carenni. I shot the bolt behind him, listened to his running footsteps—he certainly was taking me seriously enough now—and knew a brief, horrible sense of loss. But when I went back to the bed and dropped down beside Richard, all I felt was a heavenly relief. At last I could let it go.

Soon we would be back in Volterra, maybe even in Florence, with people all around us. Doctors would be examining Richard; they would say that he was going to be all right. Everything would be all right, thanks to our deliverer, to this beautiful young stranger—

I must have dozed, or half-dozed. A knock roused me, soft, but not stealthy. But it nearly made my heart jump out of my body. The sun was still shining. Surely the stranger had not been gone long enough to get help?

Was this—?

The knock came again, less softly this time. Someone—something—pushed against the door. A big, heavy body silently used its strength against that heavy wood. I sat up, shrank back an inch, and felt the warmth of Richard's unconscious body against mine. It was warm now; so was mine. But if whoever was out there should get in—

Again the massive panels shook; the hinges groaned. There was no knocking now.

The door is strong. Oh God, let it hold! Why did he have to come back now? When help would have come so soon?

Then the voice came. It said softly, "Signora, are you there?"

I could not believe my ears. I said, "Who are you?"

"Floriano Silveri. He who was with you but now."

Floriano! Somehow the name did not bring the warmth of him through the door. I moistened my lips, said, "I can't be sure of your voice. If it is you, why have you come back so soon?" A sudden thought had come to me, a ghastly and, surely, a foolish thought. I did not trust him as I had when I could see his face.

He said, "My bicycle is gone, signora. It is not in the courtyard, it is not anywhere."

So that was it. Everything was not over, the jaws of the trap were not to be so easily opened. But at least there were two of us in that trap now: myself and Floriano. My silly fear was over. That gorgeous tan of Floriano's, like a bronze statue's—no prisoner ever could have had that! Besides, how easily he could have harmed us before, when there had been no door between. I got up and opened that door for him. For Floriano.

He stepped inside quickly, looked over his shoulder once, down the silent corridor, then slammed the door and bolted it. His smile flashed at me, brilliant, beautiful as ever.

"Most profoundly do I apologize, signora! In my shock when I could not find my bike, I forgot what I myself had told you: Not to open the door until you heard my voice."

"Your bike's gone?" I had been seeing and hearing only him, but now memory came like a blow. "It will take you a lot longer, walking, won't it? I'm sorry."

He said very quietly, his dark eyes holding mine, "Signora, do you not understand? I cannot leave you now."

A minute ago I had thought that, but now I was

fully awake. "But if your bicycle's gone, he's gone! The killer!" The thought was like a sunrise.

He said soberly, "Not necessarily. We know only that he has made sure that I cannot leave."

"But you can! You can walk—"

"Signora, unless I met a car, which is not likely, you would be alone for many hours."

I shivered, then remembered that Richard was hurt. "You must go."

"Signora, I repeat that I cannot leave you alone. With, perhaps, a murderer."

"If you don't go, I must."

He said gently, "No, signora. You might be followed."

The thing I had thought of that morning, the thing that had made me feel faint then, and did again now. For a little while I did not realize that he was still talking: "...So even if the roads did not mislead you, and there were no evil behind you, you would be lost in the dark. Your husband himself would not want you to take such a mad, foolish risk."

"I know he wouldn't, but somebody's got to."

"Why? If he, that evil one, is yet here, he is watching for me to leave. When I stay beside you—a strong man—he will see that his trick has failed and go."

I swallowed. "But he'll be here when night falls. What if he comes up again?"

"He will not. We will have the lights on."

"We can't. The electricity's off."

Again he smiled. "The hall below is dark even at

midday, signora, and when I left you I thought it wise to turn on the lights. The switch is at the head of the stairs. So also is the master switch. When one brought no light, I turned on the other."

It had been so easy—so simple—and how glad I would have been of those lights last night! Yet I had never even seen those switches. I had been a hysterical fool.

"So he will know he cannot take us by surprise, signora. Though indeed he could hardly tamper with so heavy a door without giving me much warning."

"What if he is armed?"

His white teeth flashed. "You say that old Mattia's skull was smashed. That would be the work of a club. Me, I am not an old man; I can get out of the way of a club."

His eyes danced. Their exuberant masculinity challenged me. *You know well that I am not old.* He meant the two of us to be alone together all night except for the unconscious Richard. Well, I mustn't think like my grandmother, but Richard—

I said again, quietly, "My husband needs a doctor. One of us must go."

He said as quietly, "Signora, if ill came to me on that road—and in the dark any man can be taken by surprise—you and your husband would indeed be lost."

He was right; he could be followed too. I hadn't thought of that. My skin crawled. Death stalking so much life!

He laid his hand over mine. His touch, his voice, were so warm, so reassuring that they were like arms around me. "Signora, the skull of your husband is sound. I swear it."

For a blessed moment I believed him; then my mind worked again. "You're not a doctor. You can't know—"

"I know something of wounds. Set your mind at rest, signora." His smile was brilliant, masterful now; in that quiet room it seemed to flash like electricity. "Also you have no other choice, for I will neither leave you nor let you go."

CHAPTER IV

I tried to keep on arguing, but I couldn't; there was nothing I could do. He saw that he had won; he said gaily, "Have you food here, signora? You would be the better for a meal, and me, I have cycled far."

"Of course. I'll get you something." I jumped up gladly; the duties of a hostess should give me dignity, set a proper distance between us. But as I moved towards my fantastic kitchen, he moved with me. Lithely, with all a cat's grace.

We got the meal together. His slim, beautiful hands were amazingly deft and strong. With ease he twisted open a can to which I would have had to take the can opener. Sometimes his hands touched mine, but they never pressed or lingered. He found the bottle of wine Dr. Pulcinelli had given Richard as a parting gift, and though I didn't drink much of it, I am afraid I laughed as if I had. It was good, so good, not to be alone!

Around mid-afternoon we began our dessert; the shadows were lengthening. I sat facing the window, and I could see them stretching out long black arms over the green depths, turning the walled garden into a true Valley of the Shadow. Only the high white shape of Eos still towered above those dark, up-reaching tentacles.

"She is beautiful, isn't she?" I said. "It seems queer to think that last night I was afraid of her."

Floriano smiled indulgently. "If she lived she would be a thing to fear. Wings like that belong only to the great hawks."

"And to angels."

His smile broadened. "To those pretty, pious fairies the priests teach you women to believe in, signora."

That jarred me. More than I could quite understand. I said, "Angels' wings are symbolic, of course. My husband says that the early Christians probably borrowed them from your Etruscans. As perhaps they did their ideas of Hell."

His mouth tightened; a chill came over the handsome, vivid face. "So Prince Mino Carenni used to say."

"I remember. You said your family knew him?"

"As a boy, I myself had that great honor." His voice was soft, but something in the tone startled me.

"You sound as if you hadn't liked him very well."

"I like none of his caste. You Americana are forever praising the Greeks as the founders of democracy. But ancient Rome too was a republic—until those grasping, bloody-handed schemers, the Caesars, strangled it. The Italian people have always loved freedom. Like all people everywhere."

"I'm sorry. I know that's true. But Greek greatness died with Greek democracy; most of Rome's came after the republic ended. I suppose that's why we foreigners always think more about the empire."

"You are wrong, signora." His eyes blazed. "All Rome's greatness was the people's. Out of their blood, their sweat, their vigor, it was hewn. But the rotten scheming aristocrats robbed them of its fruits—they and their helpers, the greedy shopkeepers. Capitalists have always been with us."

So that was it. Nobody talks more loudly of freedom than those who have never grasped its true meaning; those who send others to death or concentration camps for not believing as they do. "I disagree with every word you say, but I will fight to the death for your right to say it." Which great early American said that, or something like that? I am ashamed to say that I can't remember, though to me his creed represents the very foundation of any world worth living in.

Well, Floriano had as much right to be a communist as I had not to be one. And he had grown up in a war-devastated country, recently ruled by Mussolini. To him Americans might still seem the victorious enemy, at best a pack of smug Santa Clauses. He certainly was the theoretical, idealistic type of communist, not the active kind that Dr. Pulcinelli had spoken of. He never could have taken part in anything like that atrocity at the ironworks. Not beautiful Floriano. Probably it would be impossible to make him believe that such a thing had ever happened.

I said peaceably, "I'm sorry again. You know your country better than I do; I'm just a tourist. But anybody can see that you're a race of artists. I'll never forget the wonderful things I saw in Florence. And that statue down there—the Eos—" I pointed toward the garden.

"She is not even an original work." His face was suddenly, shockingly hard. "Taddeo Credi copied her from the design on an Etruscan mirror, made her to Prince Mino's order. Everything Taddeo Credi ever had has always been at Prince Mino's orders. Even his beautiful daughter, Rossana."

The bitterness in his voice shocked me. Could this boy have loved a girl the prince had taken from him? No, surely not; he was too young. I said, "That sounds like the old stories of *le droit du seigneur.*"

He laughed shortly. "Noblemen never needed *le droit.* Peasant girls have very little. When offered pretty presents, they do not run fast. Or far." He brooded a moment. "Fear too. You rich Americans, you do not know how fear feels. Even when your George Dennis came here, less than a hundred years ago, to write about things Etruscan, there were still nobles who had power of life and death over the peasants. Yes, the power to kill."

Startled, I said the first thing that came into my head. "But George Dennis wasn't American. He was English."

"What difference? Save that you Americans are even richer."

Everything I said seemed to stir up a hornet's nest. I made one more effort to change the subject. "What did become of Prince Mino? Is he dead, or still in the sanitarium?"

Floriano's fork dropped. "Why do you ask? You have just been with the professor and Signora Harris; they must know."

"I wasn't with them long, and I'd barely heard of him then. I never thought of asking."

"He must be dead by now." His voice was rough. "He must be! He is sad, a weak old man who has lost everything he ever cared for."

I said, surprising myself, "Then he couldn't have hidden in our car yesterday. He wouldn't have been agile enough."

It was like a door opening in my mind, a door that I had trying to keep shut. I suddenly knew what I had been afraid of, whom I had been afraid of, all along. I found myself telling Floriano all about the escaped prisoner, about my own fantastic fear that the fugitive might have left Volterra in our car, Richard's and mine.

"It was silly, of course," I ended. "Anybody would have been frightfully uncomfortable, curled up in our car trunk. But last night, in the dark, I couldn't keep from thinking about it." I laughed, expecting him to laugh too.

But his face was troubled. "He could have been moved to the asylum. The Carenni estate may be gone; the war ruined many—even of the rich. And I heard that tumult in Volterra; it was great enough to have covered the escape of many men. It might have given a man the idea of escaping. And if he were free, he could come here. Nothing—no one—ever could stop *him*."

I felt my skin creep. "Then you think it might have been the prince, after all—?"

His brilliant smile flashed again, enveloping me like the warmth of an embrace. "Not if he had to travel in the trunk of your car. We talk folly, signora. He is an old man, and feeble, if he lives. Broken, as he deserves to be. Whoever is with us in this house tonight, it is not he."

The last words evoked a faceless image that chilled me. I said, "If somebody is here, it might be better if it were the prince. Somebody...not strong."

"Have no fear, signora. I am strong. I will protect you." His hand shot across the table and touched mine; I was still tingling from that brief, somehow intimate touch when he said, sobering swiftly, "But madmen are dangerous at any age. Do not wish for the company of one."

"You think Prince Mino really was mad?"

"Always. He was also a murderer. No doubt your husband and his friends did not tell you that; these scholars shield one another. But a young Englishman called Carstairs sought refuge here during the war. He entered the villa and was never seen again."

"I've heard about that. But I thought nobody was sure he came."

"Allied searchers found a gold pen in the cellars, signora. His name was on it. And tonight I found this."

He drew a small, stained leather notebook from his pocket. "Look at this. It must have been his. The writing is in English. And the dates are right."

The writing was in English. The first date—April 30, 1945—seemed to leap at me. I heard my own voice demanding, "Where did you get this?"

"I found it upon the flagstones, near the kitchen door. While I searched for my wheel." His voice was very grave. "Someone must have been in great haste—or in great fear—to have dropped it there. Someone must have been very clever, too, to have found what the Allied searchers could not find when they were going over the villa, inch by inch, for any trace of Roger Carstairs."

"You mean—somebody knew where to look—?" My lips were stiff.

"Because he himself had hidden it there, signora. Or had seen the killer hide it."

"Mattia Rossi! Then he was the servant who betrayed Prince Mino."

Floriano said quietly, "Yes. That much I knew already. And when I found this book, I knew that you had not imagined your dead man. And I hurried back to you."

Again his words evoked that terrible, lurking presence, that menace that even now might be creeping through the vaults below.

It could even be nearer. Perhaps listening at the door....

I thrust that image away. I said, "But if Mattia had the book, why didn't he show it? To prove his story?"

"And give up the clue that might lead to a golden treasure?" Floriano's smile was dry. "Our Tuscan peasants are shrewder than that, signora."

"But he didn't use it!"

"He could not read English. Perhaps he waited, hoping to find someone who did. Someone he could trust."

"And that person killed him? Or else"—I shivered again—"some way Prince Mino did get back—"

"Then he would have taken his revenge, calling it justice. He never doubted his right to punish." For a moment Floriano's mouth and eyes were very grim; then he relaxed. "But we have agreed that the prince cannot have come back in the flesh, signora, and surely we are not such superstitious fools as to fear his ghost. No, more likely old Mattia trusted the wrong man, was betrayed in his turn. Let us see what we can make of this diary, for that is what it seems to be. You whose native tongue is English may be able to read much that I cannot."

It was not easy reading. A great brownish stain had soaked through the book; whatever my hands touched that, I shrank away, as if from unbearable cold. But finally—using some guesswork—we did manage to piece together a fairly continuous narrative.

Roger Carstairs had come to the villa by night, crawling through thickets that normally he or any man would have thought impassable. Scratched and bleeding, he finally had come upon what he had hoped for: a hole covered by bushes, a hole that turned out to be a vertical shaft leading down into unknown depths. Such hidden vaults honeycomb the now barren Tuscan hills.

"I knew I was taking a risk, going down in there with no light, but I figured that that way I could shake off any men who might still be trailing me and find a place to rest."

Shelter he found, but also fear. This was very different from his pre-war, professional visits to such Etruscan sites. Soon he realized that he was wandering in a labyrinth at least as inexplicable as the famous cuccumella of Camars: a gigantic, uncanny spiderweb of stone passages and chambers.

"I never had been so thankful for a good mechanical memory. Right turn, left turn—fifth right turn, fifteenth left turn—it's after your counting gets up into the teens that you begin to have some doubts about the jolly old memory, after all."

Exhausted, faint with hunger, he plodded on and on down those entangling, smothering passages. The silence and the darkness were awful; he could see nothing, he could hear nothing but his own footsteps, his own heavy breathing. "Air must have been coming from somewhere, but there wasn't much of it, and it seemed to be getting worse. And when I tried to turn back, I found out there'd been some truth in the jolly old doubts. I was lost, completely lost. The harder I tried to get out, the deeper in I got."

Once, for what seemed hundreds of feet, he had to wriggle forward on his belly, feeling the stone roof above him scrape his hair. Nothing in his whole life had ever seemed so good as the moment when that pressure ceased.

But his relief did not last long. Soon all the passages began to slope sharply uphill; the only one in which he could stand upright became positively steep. He staggered on, sweat-soaked, his breath whistling, determined only to keep going until he dropped. Knowing that if—or rather, when—he would die there in the suffocating, stony dark.

Several times he fell, but managed to get up again. The last time was just within sight of another turn.

For beyond that turn, he saw a glimmer of light.

He staggered forward, shouting, burst into a room where bottle-filled shelves lined the walls. An old man yelled and dropped a pitcher of wine.

He was in Prince Mino's wine cellar. "And it looked like heaven. For hours I hadn't been able to see my hand before my face. Until you've been trapped in darkness like that, you don't know what it means to be able just to *see.*"

He fell again then, his last strength gone. "And a good thing I did too, because a man chasing you looks dangerous. A man lying on the ground doesn't." The old fellow, who had been in full flight, heard that fall and the groan that went with it; he came back to peer down into the gaunt face.

"You! You, signore!"

It was Mattia Rossi; he remembered Roger from that young man's pre-war visit to the villa, and he was quick to understand. He brought back the wine and gave him a drink.

"I will bring food too, signore. Thanks to God that here we are too deep beneath the earth for my foolish yells to have been heard! Most of us here would be glad to help you, but there is always one Judas."

The old fellow's simplicity, his kindly decency, breathe through every word that Roger Carstairs wrote. Mattia Rossi cannot have dreamed then who that Judas would be; when he did know, the knowledge must have meant heartbreak. I am sorry to think that he had to live through all those years remembering, perhaps knowing that it was he himself who unwittingly had set death to waiting, watching in the shadows.

All Roger knew then was that he was sinking comfortably, happily, into an abyss of peace. When the old man tried to raise his head and feed him, he could eat little. "Funny. I'd been so hungry. But all I wanted then was rest. Just to lie there and not move."

He slept. And woke, hours later, in a completely

strange place. A huge, circular chamber from the center of whose ceiling a grinning Gorgon's head glared down at him. Round the walls a black, hideous man-vulture, his taloned hands brandishing whips made of snakes, was chasing the terrified shapes of men and women. "For a minute I thought I'd died and gone to Hell."

Then he understood. He was in a typical late Etruscan tomb, built when the Rasenna's power was fading and their once blissful belief in an afterlife had turned into a nightmare, perhaps because they thought their gods were punishing them for some known crime. He was lying on a camp cot, in clean silk pajamas, with clean sheets over and under him. Funeral urns lined the walls and, by turning his head, he could see the sarcophagus built against the massive central pillar, beneath the glaring Gorgon's head. Here the master and mistress of some ancient household slept, their dependants around them. Their painted, life-sized effigies half-sat, half-reclined upon the sarcophagus, side by side. In the dim light, the two looked startlingly, almost threateningly alive, capable of rising to chastise an intruder.

Light! Where was it coming from? Roger raised himself on one elbow and saw the whole room. A gray-haired man sat at a folding table on which was an oil lamp strong enough to give his work full light. He was writing, his fine aquiline face set in lines of concentration. The beautiful fabric of his pinstripe gray suit looked as if he had just dressed to welcome an honored guest in his elegant drawing room.

Mattia Rossi's master—the master of all here, above ground and below! Prince Mino Carenni.

He heard Roger's movement and turned, smiling. "Welcome, signore. I hope that you are better."

"Mattia told you I was here?" Roger himself could not have explained why he felt such surprise.

"Naturally." A faint lift of the fine brows. "My servants are well trained."

"You could get into trouble for harboring me, sir."

"My dear boy, this is my house. At least it is a Carenni possession, on—or rather, under—Carenni land. Never yet has a Carenni surrendered a guest to enemies. Not even when they were civilized men of his own race, and their cause was just. I have no intention of surrendering you to barbarian invaders." The prince still smiled, but his voice was dry.

I believe now that that was true! That Prince Mino would have borne torture without betraying to the Nazis any man whom he had received as a guest. Even though Roger Carstairs never was to come up out of that underworld beneath the Villa Carenni. Never again to see the sun....

Roger himself had no doubts whatsoever. "The Prince is a fine old boy; he's being jolly decent. Couldn't be doing more for me if he were my own father. Makes me ashamed to remember how, before the war, we young fellows used to think him such a queer fish."

He liked and trusted his host at first; so much is clear. Certainly it never occurred to him that his diary might be read; but it was read, I think, from the very beginning. One stained page rather pathetically records his gratitude for the gift of the little leather notebook, made with one of Prince Mino's most gracious smiles. "I remember that you write. Perhaps this will help to pass the time."

"The time! There is no time down here. You can't tell day from night. The kind of food old Mattia brings— breakfast, lunch, dinner—that's your only clue."

Writing did help. But when he had slept off his fatigue, Roger grew restless. Inexplicably uneasy too.

On May 14th he wrote: "Had breakfast. That seems to be all there is to say. I take exercises, I've got to keep fit, but I've had to slack up on even those. One day I took too many and got a crick in my back that crippled me for a couple of days. For the time it took old Mattia to bring six meals down, anyhow.

"Even a clock would be company down here; it would tick. You have to live in a place like this before you know what silence is. Real silence, not all the funny mess of tiny sounds that goes by that name up above. There's nothing alive down here, in all this stone; it doesn't shelter bugs, or make little snaps, the way wood does. Sometimes the silence seems as loud as a yell. Makes me feel like kicking the furniture and yelling too."

I know how you felt, Roger Carstairs. Since I came to the Villa Carenni, I too have learned how loud silence can be. How very loud.

"May 17th: I hate to ask for anything more; the old boy's already done so much for me—but a clock would help. If I could count the time—just say, 'This twelve hours is noon, that one's midnight'—I could keep in touch with reality. Where there's so much silence, it oughtn't to be so easy to imagine sound."

It had begun. Death had come, creeping, spying, on perhaps not quite noiseless feet....

Then: "May 20th: I think it's that. Yesterday—I suppose it was yesterday, I've slept since then—Prince Mino came and I asked him for a clock. He said, 'I am sorry that a guest of mine should be bored, but if I took one from its place the servants would wonder and talk among themselves.' I said I understood, and he said, 'I had hoped that books might entertain you. But youth—even scholarly youth—craves action, excitement.' He wasn't quite pleased.

"I said I'd had enough of both to last me a lifetime; what ailed me now was nerves, and I'd soon adjust. 'As for books, it's a great privilege to have access to yours, sir. Any real scholar would give a year of his life for my chance at them.' He smiled at that, and was completely friendly again, more so than I'd ever seen him. 'I hope that you will always think so, my young friend. I had not known that you English were such courtiers.'

"It wasn't flattery, and I told him so. Libraries that have books like his keep them under lock and key. For a while we talked so hard that we forgot everything else. He really opened up, told me his own pet theories.

"'You know—who does not?—that civilization is said to have begun in the ancient Near East. Yet though it appears later in Egypt, it already wears a somewhat superior form. Why, if a civilizing "Pre-Dynastic Race" brought it from the East, as some say?'

"I said, 'Perhaps the native Egyptian genius had already improved it before we find traces of it, sir.'

"'No. The same race that brought it to the banks of the Nile had already carried an earlier stage of it to the banks of the Euphrates. All growth, all improvement, took place among the original culture-bearers. Among people of the pure ancient blood.'

"I remembered then some of the reasons why we'd thought him a queer fish. I asked him, as tactfully as I could, if he had any idea just who those original culture-bearers could have been.

"'I know. And soon I will prove it.' His eyes blazed; he looked like an exultant fanatic. 'Did not Plato say that Atlanteans once occupied the Tyrrhene coast? Whether the place that in his Greek foolishness he called Atlantis lies beneath the sea, or—as is more likely—beneath the sands of the Sahara, that land was the cradle-land, the birthplace of all the arts of man. The birthplace of the Rasenna.'

"I was startled. 'But I thought they came from a place called Tyrrha, sir. Somewhere in Asia Minor.'

"'There they rose again after the disaster that destroyed their earlier home. From there they came to Italy—yes, a fugitive starving remnant of them came to teach the Western savages as once they had taught those earlier savages of Egypt and Sumer. Their civilization was the ancestor, the creator of all. None before or since, anywhere in the world, but has sprung from it.'

"I stared, then ventured feebly, 'What about the New World civilizations, sir? The Mayas and the Incas?'

"'Do not the Atlantic currents lead straight from the Mediterranean to Central America? To the place where the Mayas kept a calendar that dated back to a time thousands of years before the building of their own cities? Did not the Maya also wear feather crowns like those of ancient warriors of the Near East? Those ignorant savages who entered America through the Bering Strait—there were many pleasant lands in which they could have stopped to build cities before they reached Central America. Why there—amid deserts and jungles—did they suddenly learn how to build? Why?'

"I said truthfully, 'I don't know why.'

"'Then think why! The Phoenicians fought with the Rasenna for a western 'Isle of Refuge.' I say that some of the Rasenna reached that isle, and went on to become teachers in the wild lands beyond, even as they had already taught all other civilized peoples in the world.'

"He stopped for breath, but his eyes still shone. 'The Rasenna were the torch-bearers, the creators, born to lead all mankind. Had they kept their heritage pure—

not been corrupted by Greek wordiness, absurd Greek dreams of democracy—they would have built the empire that their bastard heirs, the Romans, built. But they would have held it. We would now be living in a sane and ordered world. Not in chaos—not in a mad, mechanized jungle where no man has time to enjoy beauty and the arts for frenziedly devising ways to kill his neighbor before that neighbor kills him.'

"He paused, searching my face for an answering light. I think I only looked bewildered and a little troubled, and his own face changed subtly. I wish it hadn't."

CHAPTER V

"The old chap is mad," Roger wrote. "But at least it's a relief to hear of a master-race that isn't blond."

"I'm ashamed to say it, but I wish I had played up to him. He might have let a convert work with him. He is doing some sort of work in a place even deeper in the earth than this; he's never made any secret of that. And I don't think he's unbalanced enough to have said so positively, 'I will soon prove it,' if he hadn't found something. There are scraps of old tradition about early Etruscans in Egypt. Who knows? I might have been able to help him, to put his discovery on a sound scientific basis. And Lord knows I need something to do."

For several days Prince Mino did not come again. And in his loneliness Roger began to imagine things, or to think he did.

On May 24th he wrote: "I am nervy; all this black wilderness of stone around my own snug little tomb gets me. I'm afraid that part of my desire to explore it is really desire to prove that there's nothing moving in it. That all the spooks are painted on the walls.

"So often I feel that there's something in the darkness, just beyond the light of my lamp. Something watching me. The other morning—if it was morning— I woke up thinking I heard footsteps. And this book was lying open, though I'd have sworn I shut it before I went to bed. That was one of my bad mornings, too; sometimes I sleep too hard and wake up feeling rotten. It must be the air down here."

Or was something being added to your trays, Roger? Slipped into your coffee, perhaps, while some casual-seeming remark made old Mattia look the other way? It must have been done deftly, cunningly, so that Mattia never knew.

Roger never knew, either. His next entry shows how good sense can blind a man.

"May 25th: I'm glad I wrote that yesterday; seeing it down in black and white shows me just how big a fool I've been making of myself. I need exercise, real exercise. If I took a nice long walk, nobody would ever know. If the prince comes, he always comes not long after Mattia has served my meals. Going would be so confounded easy! But it wouldn't be cricket. Bluebeard's wife was lucky; she had the run of his castle, except for one room. I've got to stay in just this one. The second time I saw him—when my legs were still wobbly—Prince Mino cautioned me about that. Very politely. 'You would run no risk of meeting my servants; only Mattia ever descends to this level. But you could easily become lost; also if the Germans should return, we would need to be able to find you quickly.'

"I said, 'If they should come, you'd better just let Mattia lead me out onto the hillside, sir. I wouldn't want to get you into trouble.' But he smiled, rather grimly.

"'No such violation of my hospitality will be necessary. Should the Germans penetrate too far into these vaults, they will encounter a small landslide. As Sulla's men encountered a large one when that Roman butcher was besieging Volterra and thought to plunder the temple here. The priests of that day had to bury themselves with their treasure, but I have had time to lay my plans. To place explosives at strategic points. None of the treasures of this most ancient and holy shrine of the Rasenna ever will go to adorn the blond savages' so-called museums in Berlin.'

"I jumped. 'You mean you've got explosives down here? They're risky stuff to handle, sir. You might blow up a lot more than you intended to.'

"For just a second, icy wrath stiffened my host's face. 'You think I do not understand what I do? What I guard will be buried, not destroyed. My explosions— if any—will be carefully sized and timed. Only barbarians will die; a civilized man can always outwit such as them.'

"I thought, 'I hope you know as much about explosives as you think you do,' but I had too much sense to say so. And after that he was very pleasant again; we had a good evening. I'm sorry if I did offend the old fellow the other day; I miss him. Besides, I owe him a lot; I certainly should consider his feelings."

On the twenty-seventh, Prince Mino did come back. The first part of the entry is lost, drowned in that brown stain, and from there on there is never a clear page, but I think we made out most of that scene. We had to start in the middle of a sentence. "...beginning to seem like my own tomb, sir. You've made me very comfortable here, but I must say these wall paintings would make almost anybody afraid of death." Roger must have been looking at that vulture-demon, with his serpent-whip.

"But that was wisely arranged." Prince Mino's smile was tolerant. "The early Rasenna went dancing into battle. No race ever had a more fiery lust for life, but by teaching them to expect bliss after death, their priest-kings made them fearless warriors. Later, in their decline, when they had lost hope and desired only to drowse pleasantly toward death, then priests who were no longer kings had to make death terrible. The common people must always be told what to believe."

"The fear treatment doesn't seem to have worked." Roger evidently couldn't resist saying that.

"Because they had turned from their warrior kings; because Greek democracy had emasculated them. Democracy!" Prince Mino's lip curled. "That never has lasted long anywhere. In Greece, its birthplace, it endured but a moment. In lands whose fat merchants are guarded by the sea, like your Britain and America, it soon will go down before planes and submarines. Young men like you should face that fact, make sounder plans for the future."

Roger seems to have said slowly, "Any man would be a fool to try to say what this world will be like by 1990, sir. But this I do know: without democracy, it won't be a place I'll enjoy living in."

"We disagree." Prince Mino shrugged. "You think the people rule you. Your money-loving shopkeepers really do: men without taste or fineness. Fascism, if intelligently directed, could have saved the world. Mussolini had a gleam of real vision, one his poor peasant's brain could never execute. Only those are fit to rule whose ancestors have ruled before them; judgment, true leadership, require both breeding and heredity. A base-born dog like Benito presumed too far when he dared to take as his own symbol the Etruscan axe—the *fasces*. He should have been whipped back to his kennel then."

"We democrats are trying to do that now, sir."

"To what end? Stop this precious pair—the butcher's son and the housepainter—and more louts will rise. You lack the wit to keep such ruffians in their native gutters. Such foolishness comes of a faith that believes its God actually to have incarnated himself in a carpenter's son."

Roger says that he never had thought of himself as a religious man, yet that shocked him. He said bluntly,

"Like a good many other scholars—better known ones—I feel that their religion ruined your Rasenna, sir. Their belief that their race had to pass away at the end of a certain number of cycles."

Prince Mino stiffened. "Each of those cycles could have lasted a thousand years. Or ten thousand. Corruption ruined the Rasenna; the poison they sucked in from the lower races. There was no flaw in the laws Tarchon laid down for his people."

"Tarchon, sir? I thought Tages was the law-giver—the gray-haired boy-god who rose out of the Earth."

Prince Mino smiled gently. "Are you too naive to understand that myth? The boy must have been carefully chosen and coached. Silver-gilt was put on his hair, and he must have had some good blood to learn his lessons so well. Bastards can sometimes have great beauty, show great promise—yet if the mother is low-born, the promise always fails." His face had darkened; for a moment his voice held bitterness, even pain.

"Tarchon understood that. After giving his people the laws that their king wrote down, the boy-god returned into the Earth, remember. In other words, he was buried, having been quietly smothered or poisoned. A wise ruler is unsentimental."

"You think he was Tarchon's own child?" Roger was startled.

"Assuredly. Sons can be dangerous, yet a man needs them. A race must have them. By papal dispensation I married my cousin, a gentle and lovely lady, but she had only the fineness of our stock, not its vigor. She lived for many years but she bore no child, and in those days I was myself too sentimental to take the needed steps. Yet probably it did not matter; one man's progeny could scarcely have given a race rebirth."

"He was thinking out loud then," Roger wrote, "not really talking to me. To have no son must be a great grief to a man like that. For him there's no future. Hitler has (or had) plenty of hopes for his appalling race of super-men (super-bullies, rather), but for the prince everything that exists or that ever can exist is paltry beside his dead-and-gone Rasenna. Wonder what he'd think if he could go back in time and see them as they were. Some Roman playwright accused the women of earning their dowries by prostitution, I remember—the way the Ouled Nail still do in North Africa. But the prince probably would say that that was a foul slander, envious Roman women's gossip. Etruscan ladies were famous for their beauty. I have a feeling that his highness isn't exactly the man to be broad-minded about women."

At that line Floriano laughed. Suddenly and harshly. "He was not altogether a fool, that Englishman!"

There was not much more of the entry left. "...I'm sorry for the old chap; his can't be a cheerful obsession. But I've got to get out of this room occasionally, or I'll soon be going queer myself."

There anything like coherent narrative ends. Roger may have begun by going just a little way from his tomb-chamber. One turn, two turns the first day, perhaps—then more. The desire to explore inevitably whetted, inevitably growing.

He went farther and farther. Not without qualms.

"...any noise doubly loud in a place like this... own footsteps sound like two men's...I'd have sworn someone behind me. Conscience? I'm not disturbing anything...never speak of anything I've seen with(out) host's leave, of course."

A few fragments draw a dreadful picture. "...damned ugly sight.... Wish I had stayed in my room today.... A good old Etruscan punishment, of course; Virgil mentions it; and all of them must have been proud of their Etruscan blood, even if they weren't obsessed by it, like Prince Mino. God knows what obsessed or possessed a man who could do a thing like that...heard the yarn years ago: How, whenever an heir of the Carenni comes of age, his father brings him down to see those two skeletons...lesson against treachery. And Prince Mino calls other people barbarians.... Never dreamed the thing could be true, but here they are!... Old saying about everybody having some skeleton in his closet, but those two—!"

Bewildered, I looked at Floriano. "Have you any idea what he's talking about?

He looked surprised. "You do not know the story? How young Amedeo Carenni loved his father's bride?"

A horrible thought came to me. "You mean that girl the villa was rebuilt for—?"

"She. Her husband caught her and his son together."

"And then the boy's own father killed him?"

"As he lay in his beloved's arms. And she—that daughter of the people who had been bought from her humble parents like a cow—was chained living to his corpse and buried with him. That is the good old Etruscan punishment our friend spoke of." Floriano's mouth was grim; his eyes smoldered. "They say the old man said to her, 'I will be kind. Since you wished to lie with my son, you shall do so until your bones crumble.' And so it was done—that kindness of the Carenni!"

"Are you sure? I thought—my husband said nobody really knew what had happened—" I felt sick.

"When Prince Mino himself came of age, his father took him down into the vaults to see them. It is indeed a ritual with the heir of the Carenni. 'The most noble and proud Carenni.'"

"How horrible!"

"But such horror as the pride and power of those old families made possible. That a young girl should be kept prisoner in this lonely place to serve an old man's lust—a few words mumbled by a priest made that right, respectable. But that youth should turn to youth—that was sin. Shame and treachery. A crime that deserved the worst of punishments."

"And got it. The death that girl died! Slowly, in the dark—" My voice broke.

"She got off easily. She had betrayed one Carenni, and corrupted another. Women who betrayed that sacred breed more recently have died more slowly. Uglier deaths." The bitterness in his voice cut like a knife. "Prince Mino was no better than his ancestors, signora. Never think that. Never forget the kindness of the Carennis."

"For a moment I wondered just what he was talking about, then sheer horror caught me again. "You said 'uglier deaths.' What could be worse? That poor girl—down there in the dark—"

I suppose it was because I was so very tired, had been under a strain for so long, but I suddenly began to cry. I kept on crying, out of plain panic, just because I was ashamed of myself for doing it. Floriano moved towards me and I wondered if he was going to slap me, as hysterical heroines in books and plays get slapped. I stepped back, quickly, sank into a chair.

"It's all right. I'm all right."

He halted. Did a shade of disappointment, of something uglier, cross that beautiful face? Make it momentarily less beautiful? It passed; he shrugged.

"But it could be much better, signora. Me, I am told that I have a good shoulder for beautiful ladies to cry on."

No doubt, I thought. I said, "Better not let married women use it too much. Remember Amedeo." And laughed again. For another panicky second I thought that that laughter too was going to go on and on. Thank goodness, it didn't.

"At least Amedeo and that girl knew joy before they

died, signora." His eyes met mine; their warmth was like a physical touch.

"I hope it was worth it."

It hadn't been; I knew that. Not worth the hunger and the thirst, the smell of dead flesh rotting beside her in the blackness. Flesh that had been strong and beautiful and loving, perhaps as beautiful as Floriano's.... Had she finally turned and torn it before she died? Had that been the old devil's plan?

"Had she lived, she would have suffered far more. With the old man sleeping beside her every night." Floriano's voice was very gentle; he might have been reading my thoughts. "He outlived her by ten years. She did well to enjoy her youth as best she could."

He was closer than I had thought, close beside me. I snatched at any way to change the subject. "Hadn't we better finish the diary? There can't be much of it left."

He rose to that bait, much more quickly than I had expected. "Yes."

There wasn't much left, but what there was soon became electrifying. There is nothing to show how or when Roger Carstairs made his great discovery, but make it he did.

"Schliemann never found such treasure at Troy, nor Evans at Knossos.... Masses...brought here from many palaces and temples, one by one...cities fell before the Romans. He's labeled some...from...fabled shrine or two-sexed Veltha, whose site nobody knows, though for ages the Rasenna from all Twelve Cities gathered there yearly.... Never has been...discovery like this. Never... can't keep his secret, such treasure belongs to all men everywhere. But how the devil will I ever make the old fellow understand...feel damned ungrateful...."

And then the blow had fallen. When it was struck, the diary must have been open. What was now an ugly brownish dullness had gushed out across the paper, red and wet. Across that paper on which Roger Carstairs had been writing his last words.

I said softly, shivering a little, "So that was it."

Floriano did not seem to hear me. "It is still there!" His eyes were blazing. "Still somewhere down there."

I was disgusted. "Whatever is down there, it wasn't worth a man's life."

"You say that, a woman! Have you ever seen Etruscan jewelry? The wonder of it, the shining golden wonder!"

"He may have meant statues, vases. To archaeologists, treasure doesn't have to mean gold."

He laughed. "The Romans carried off Veltha's own image—the thing the Etruscans held holiest! Only the things fleeing men could carry under their cloaks could have been saved. Small things, slim things. Gold!"

"I see. Perhaps you're right."

He rushed on as if he had not heard me. "I have heard Prince Mino say that in a coffer at the foot of Veltha's image, golden tablets lay. Tablets on which were engraved Tages's words that Tarchon wrote down. The dirty kingly plotter pretending to take dictation from his little stooge! Poor little parrot, trained to recite his lesson and then doomed to have his neck wrung for his obedience."

He could pity poor little long-dead Tages, whose murder he could fit into his political philosophy; he seemed already to have forgotten that of Roger Carstairs. Probably Prince Mino had seen that only as the execution of a traitor, a would-be thief, necessary and just. I felt a sick revulsion against both men, prince and communist. I said shortly, "We don't even know that Tages ever lived. And what if those tablets were gold? The inscriptions on them would be worth far more than anything they could possibly be made of."

He snorted, "Dirty propaganda worth more because it is old! I would be glad to melt them with my own hands—those lies that were graven there to enslave men! But the jewelry—the wonderful, shining jewelry—"

His own flushed face shone, virile red lips parted, dark eyes glowing. His beauty was dazzling. I thought, touched, *It isn't the money value he's thinking of. It's the beauty he loves, as innocently as a child would. The sheer beauty of all those golden, sparkling things.*

No, he was not callous. The vision of all that buried splendor had simply shut everything else out of his head. In that too he was like a child; and I was glad. The pressure of that warm male magnificence, whose pull any two-legged female must have felt, was lifted from me. His consciousness of me had faded.

I said, thinking aloud, "Prince Mino killed Roger, but why didn't he take the diary? I can't imagine him leaving it around for Mattia Rossi or anyone else to find."

"Mattia must have found it after the Allies took his master away." Floriano spoke quickly, too quickly. I had again that queer feeling that he was afraid.

"But if he couldn't read it, why should he think it would help him to find the treasure? Which it wouldn't, really."

"He must have heard Prince Mino speak words that made him think so." But Floriano spoke without conviction; he muttered, after a moment's silence, "He cannot be here. He cannot."

But just then I had what I thought was an inspiration; I felt like a fool for not having had it hours before.

"Professor Harris's desk! There must be papers there—maybe keys. It's the only place where I haven't looked for keys! The papers might record Prince Mino's death. And if we could lock those cellar doors, couldn't you risk going for help? Though I don't believe anybody's down there. That book certainly didn't give him any map to the treasure."

The murderer had dropped it because he found it useless, I thought, *the information it held unimportant beside his need to flee from the scene of his crime.* And now this queer, inexplicable fear of Floriano's gave me an advantage; because of his dread of a feeble old man, he might just possibly leave the villa.

For a moment he stood thinking. "There are no windows in the cellar. A man down there would be trapped.... And you are right; very likely he is gone. But first let us search the good professor's desk."

We did. We found the keys in the first drawer we opened. One by one I tried them in the hall door while Floriano ransacked the professor's papers. I felt guilty about letting him do that, but I didn't know how to prevent it. The keys seemed unimportant now, but handling them gave me something to do, and for more than one reason I was nervous.

I had just found the right key—the prize that would have meant so much a few hours ago—when an exclamation from Floriano made me turn.

"Prince Mino *is* here, signora!" Exultation, terrible triumph, flamed in his eyes. "Here. Below us."

I shrank back, but he rose and came toward me. His face glowed; his bright smile was back. Now all of him blazed like a flame.

"Have no fear." His hand closed on my arm. "He will not come creeping up those dark stairs when night comes. He will stay quietly where he is. As quietly as all the others."

"You don't mean—"

"See!" He thrust a letter at me. "This is what the good doctor in charge of the sanitarium wrote to our good professor. Read it. No, I forgot. You cannot read Italian, I must read it to you."

It was a little while before I began to catch the words. "...thank you for your help in fulfilling the last wishes of the late Prince Carenni. Also for your kind inquiries concerning the last days of so distinguished (and unjustly calumniated) a gentleman. They were calm; for months we had known that the end must be near, and, thanks to God, I was able to spare him pain. His courage never faltered; but although he had no religious belief and refused the services of a priest, he could not entirely shake off the ancestor worship of his forefathers. A week before his death he said to me, 'One urn among many there; that is my right. If there were consciousness after death, I should be unable to rest elsewhere. And even there, I believe—I who thought I knew how foolish was the idea of survival—I should not rest if ever the hands of vandals should disturb those most ancient holy places of my people. Somehow I should rise to avenge them.' And then he smiled and said, 'Forgive a sick old man's fancies.' But well I know that, thanks to your good care, nothing of the sort will ever trouble him where he lies beneath the house of his ancestors, in that rock chamber of his own choosing."

So that was that; the ghost was laid. No incredibly nimble old man had hidden in the trunk of Richard's car yesterday. No incredibly nimble old madman was hiding down there now, red-handed, in his own cellars.

But somebody's feet had trodden the stones of that cellar floor. Somebody had killed old Mattia Rossi. Who?

No matter. All that really mattered now was that Floriano was not going to go for help. I felt that in my bones, knew it with a sickening certainty.

CHAPTER VI

"He did not know what was coming, signora." Floriano smiled as he laid the paper down.

"Who didn't?" For a second I had forgotten Prince Mino.

He did not seem to hear me. Behind him the windows blazed red with the last of the sunset. I thought it must be the reflected light that made his eyes fiery.

"What fools, all of them! The noble prince and the good doctor, all your learned archaeologists too. The treasure *is* here. And so is the treasure-seeker! Walking over his bones—over the great, proud Prince Mino's! And he will not rise from his ashes. He cannot rise. He can do nothing, that proud one, but lie there. Not even knowing. By the God that is not"—Floriano's fist struck the table as if it were living flesh—"I wish he could know!"

I didn't understand. I said stupidly, "You think the murderer is still here then? That he didn't leave on your wheel?" But I was glad that his assault on the table had made him let go of my arm.

He smiled again, gaily, slyly. "Probably he did. But certainly Prince Mino will never trouble us. The dead do not walk. Let us think of pleasanter things."

Before I could move, he had me; his arms tight about me, his kisses coming hard and fast upon my mouth. His hunger was a contagion. That was the horrible part; I was no longer myself. Not Barbara, Richard's wife, not even a woman; only a mindless female stripped of all individuality, and so of dignity, the thing that only one's own individual worth can give.

"No—no!" I tried to pull away, to push him away, but he held me too tightly. He was talking now, spacing his words with lighter, gentler kisses, his voice as soft as velvet. "Let us be happy. Now. Before night comes. The long night that swallows up even the proud Prince Carennis. Let us be happy first, carissima."

I should have laughed at him, have told him to find some more cheerful way of seducing me, but in that place such words seemed natural enough. Besides, I was afraid. Could Floriano be made to believe that any woman, once he had had her, could feel unhappy and ashamed? He would think her bound to respond at the last instant....

"No!" I was still trying to fight him, but I could only squirm ingloriously, like a hooked fish. "My husband—"

He laughed. "That one? He lies there like a stick or

a stone. He cannot enjoy your beauty now; what right has he to begrudge it to a man who can? Is a beautiful woman property, like a horse or a dog? Do I not please you? All these hours your eyes have been telling me so. And now your mouth...."

He kissed me again. For another degrading moment the whole world seemed to be burned away. Then I only felt sick and cold and ashamed. Could it be true? Ever since he came, had I been wanting this?

I had stopped struggling, and he thought I was ready. His hands shot downward, to my dress. I sprang back so sharply that I tore away from him. He leapt after me, delighted, white teeth flashing, and caught me again.

"No! no!"

"Yes, yes, bellissima!"

Since I couldn't get away I went limp. "You don't understand."

"What do I not understand?" He rubbed his cheek against mine. "Chastity—that nonsense with which the Church, that old servant of wealth and power, fills the heads of you women? So that proud, high-born men like the Carenni can feel sure that their own rotten blood flows in the veins of those who inherit their lands and wealth?"

"Richard—my husband—and I love each other. We don't think about things like property or bloodlines."

"It is love, then, that I do not understand?" His cheek still rubbed mine, his bright eyes teased me tenderly.

"I could teach you a great deal about love, carissima. I do not think you know much about it yet."

Once again he kissed me, but this time my blood did not make that automatic, shaming response. He should not have sneered at Richard's lovemaking.

I said, "I don't belong to Richard, but I do belong to myself. You have no right to force me."

"Force you? *I?*" He stiffened, startled. "I only try to make you understand that you want me as I want you."

He crushed me to him, whispering, caressing me with his hands as I never had dreamed that a man could caress a woman. I said at last, trying to keep my voice from trembling, "Please. It isn't fair. You're so much stronger, and I'm so tired."

He let me go. I went somewhat shakily to a chair, and quite literally dropped into it. I closed my eyes, trying in that foolish way to shut him out, to be alone.

I heard him go to the table, heard the clink of glasses. Then he turned back to me, and I tensed. My eyes flew open, and the look in them must have shocked him, for he stopped where he was.

"Have no fear, signora. I will not touch you. But this"—he held out a wine glass—"will help. It is most true that you are tired. Too tired for love."

His pride and assurance were all gone. He was looking at me as a little boy with no money in his pockets might look into a shop window full of candy. And suddenly, ridiculously, I felt so sorry for him that my throat ached. He could not understand; he could not see how what he wanted could hurt either Richard or me.

I said, "It's all right, Floriano. So long as you don't do it again."

"Take this, signora." He had stepped closer, still holding out the glass. Though softly spoken, the words were a command. Instinctively I reached out my hand, then dropped it. Aren't hypnotists sometimes supposed to begin their work subtly, by giving little commands that are not likely to be disobeyed? Casual-seeming commands? More ordinarily, he could be trying to get me drunk. The idea of having to force a woman would hurt his pride, but there were other ways, and I had no doubt he knew them all.

Then I met his eyes; those beautiful dark eyes, troubled and unhappy now, and my suspicions seemed unfair, absurd. Not to drink seemed unkind, and I didn't want to be unkind. I wanted to do something for him. Anything in the world but that one thing.

I took the glass and started to drink.

Something made me look up; I saw his eyes watching me. Assured again, gloatingly expectant...and I knew. He might be innocent in his way, but so is the tiger that stalks the jungle at twilight; he only wants his evening meal.

The glass fell and broke; the wine splashed all over my dress. I cried out. Floriano reached for a paper napkin, but I pushed it away. "No, that's not big enough. Get me a towel. A wet towel—"

He vanished into the bathroom. I took one long, heartsick look towards that inner room in which Richard lay; then I sprang up and ran for the hall door. It seemed miles away. How easy it would be for Floriano to dart back through one door before I could get out at the other! My heart lurched sickeningly. I heard the sound of a faucet running; Floriano must be holding the towel under it. I never had dreamed that the noise a faucet makes could be music to my ears, but nothing has ever sounded sweeter. Through that he could hear no ordinary sound I might make.

I was at the hall door. I was through it and into the hall! I had the key in my pocket; thank God that I had put it there! But how long can it take to get a key out of one's pocket? There! I had it. I must not drop it—I must not—

And then I heard him—his shout, his rush on the other side of the door I had just closed! I plunged the key into the lock; just as his weight crashed into the heavy panels, it turned. They shook, but their ancient might held firm. It was as if all elaborately carved figures that covered them had risen to my defense, were holding him back. I heard another cry, and it was not like any sound that I ever had thought could come from Floriano's throat.

I ran downstairs, that beast cry still ringing in my ears. "He can't get out!" I kept telling myself that. The lack of trees and vines near the windows would keep him in, just as I had counted on its keeping the murderer out.

The great front doors loomed before me, slammed behind me. I ran through the courtyard, and fell headlong over something that lay there. Hard leather saddle edges cut my chest. Floriano's bicycle! It was what lay there, exactly where I had first seen it. He never had believed my story, had only invented one of his own as an excuse to stay with me.

Well, you may get a surprise, Floriano. I hope not, for Richard's sake. But to defend yourself, you must defend him too. If the murderer comes, he will attack the man who is awake.

I was out of the courtyard now, running down the road, the breeze fresh in my face. My bruised chest ached and throbbed, but I was out of the Villa Carenni, out of all its terrors and traps. In the open, where there was no shelter to hide a pursuer.

My exultation didn't last long. Soon my run slowed to a plodding walk; the road stretched terribly, desolately, before me. I remembered how long and lonely a way Richard and I had come—was it only yesterday? I never would be able to make it unless I met another car.

Keep going, keep going, keep watching. All my tiredness seemed to come upon me at once, like a physical weight. I wanted to cry.

That was when I saw it—not another road, nothing that we Americans, used to super-highways, would ever think of as a road—but a kind of track, leading up into the hills. The way to the village! It must be that.

That track wasn't easy to follow. Several times I

stumbled and nearly fell again. From continually looking back over my shoulder. The sky was bright now, with afterglow, but soon night would fall. There might be a moon, but that would help my possible pursuer too. If only I could be sure the murderer was down in the vaults, busy with his treasure-hunting!

If he was above ground, if he knew I had gone, he must be following me. The person who had left the villa would represent the greatest threat to him.

But gradually fear of pursuit faded, crowded out by sheer physical misery. The track rose steadily upwards; the hills closed in around me, silent, purple, without a sign of life upon them. The climb was hard. I was swaying a little as I went, panting. *One step more, just one step more—you don't have to think about the next step until this one's taken. Keep going; just keep going.*

I couldn't stop to rest. I must be within sight of the village before night came. I never could see to follow that track in the dark.

I reached the top of a hill. From it I could see other hills, dark against the graying sky. I strained my eyes; hadn't Richard said that unless you looked closely, you couldn't see some of those old Tuscan villages from a distance? They had grown out of—and into—those hills that had held them from time immemorial.

It was there. Thank God, it was there! Smoke curling up darkly into that faded evening sky. Even in midsummer heat, the people here have to light fires to cook.

That last climb will not bear remembering. Once I did stop; surely it wouldn't hurt to rest a little now; I was so near. A last flicker of caution made me look behind me, down those slopes where shadows were massing.

Did one shadow move?

I held my breath. I must have been wrong. No! One of the shadows was moving. A shadow too tall to be a stray goat's....

I scrambled up and ran. *It may be just the goatherd. It may be just any villager, coming home.* I kept telling myself that, but I never believed myself.

Once I slowed down enough to look back. The shadow was no longer there, but a dark figure was climbing steadily, purposefully, behind me.

But now I could see strange, steep old houses rising up ahead of me. Could I reach them before that dark figure reached me? With a final burst of speed, I ran, ran as I never had run before. Every gasping, sobbing breath seemed to tear my lungs.

I was stumbling between pigsties now. I tripped over one pig and fell headlong into filth. I got up and nearly ran into some other moving object—heard a child scream.

I swerved and ran on, came out onto what must be the village main street. A dirt track that ran between houses, out onto the cliffs. I was there! I was there!

The child I had nearly knocked down was still screaming, dogs that looked half-starved were yapping, and now other children began to scream and run. Men stared at me, their jaws dropping. Women stared too, women whose dark dresses and still, carved faces made them look more like birds of prey than fellow women who might understand and help me.

"*Aita! Aita!*" I stopped and moaned, throwing out my hands in the age-old gesture of supplication.

But all of them only stood there, staring. Suspicious, hostile, wondering. I had frightened their children, I had brought commotion into their quiet. Also the filthy, scarecrow figure I made by then cannot have looked quite human, and there is a terrible, world-wide delusion that that is just what foreigners are. Not quite people, not like oneself, ourselves.

I tried to pull myself together, to speak calmly. "Does anyone here understand English? Even a few words of it? I need help—*aita. Por favore*—please!"

Everywhere in Florence there had been people who spoke English. I had been told that even in the smaller towns, there was always someone who had been to America, or who had worked in the cities, and picked up a few words of it. Mrs. Harris must have been wrong; even in this tiny mountain hamlet, there must be someone who could understand that I was in trouble, needed help.

But they only stood and stared. Some eyes narrowed a little, puzzled; that was all.

I tried again. "My husband is hurt. *Mio marito—aita.* And someone is following me. I'm afraid. Afraid!"

I shouldn't have said that last; it let the note of panic

creep back into my voice. Made me seem outside reason again, like a wild animal that would be dangerous if it could.

I said loudly—why is it always so easy to behave as if foreigners were deaf? *"Mio marito! Aita! Aita!* (My husband! Help! Help!)" If only I had known some word for "hurt" or "injured."

Still no answer, only that wall of watchful faces. I wanted to batter it with my hands, as I might have battered a real wall. I had tried so hard to reach them, and now that I was here among them, I could not. The gulf of language yawned between us, impassable.

I lost control of myself and screamed at them. "English! English! English! Go get somebody who understands it! Please. *Please!"*

Still they only stood there, their faces hard, uncomprehending, like those of people on a frieze. To them I was only making unintelligible noises, as a maddened animal might.

The voice came from behind me then, speaking Italian. Quietly, reassuringly—I could not understand the words, but I understood the tone. Something else about that voice, a man's voice, made my heart stand still. I could not believe my ears.

All those carving-like faces were breaking up into humanity, into smiles and friendliness. They were moving, the people were making way for someone who was coming. I swung round to see.

I couldn't believe my eyes either. He couldn't be

there; it must be someone else. He was very near; some people were smiling at him and speaking to him. Plainly they knew him; and I didn't have to know their language to know what they were thinking: *Here is someone who will know what to do.*

He was beside me now, he smiled and spoke to me, he tried to lay his hand on my arm, but I jerked away from him.

He said in English, very gently and kindly, as if he were saying the friendliest thing in the world, "Did you think you could get away, you fool? Outwit me here, in my own hills?"

I suppose I did the worst possible thing then. I shrieked, neither in English, nor in Italian. The cry came from a level of consciousness too deep, too primitive, for language.

He grabbed me. I was in his arms, twisting, scrabbling, scratching, trying to claw his face. I must have looked completely mad. No villagers anywhere in the world would have tried to stop what he did then.

Floriano's fist darting towards my jaw and Floriano's beautiful, smiling face behind it, those were the last things I saw before the world went out in a shower of stars.

CHAPTER VII

Darkness, creaking, jolting darkness. Something pricked me when I moved; whatever I was lying on was rough. Where was I?

Then Floriano's beautiful face burned through the darkness, vivid as if it were still there before me. Telling me again what it had told me in that last terrible moment. I bit my lips until they bled.

Richard! I had left Richard alone with a murderer.

Somehow Floriano had gotten out to follow me. But first had he turned and vented his rage on the unconscious man? No, surely not; surely all his energies had been bent on contriving his escape, on his pursuit of me. Yet sickeningly I remembered old Mattia Rossi's gray hair blood-matted on the gray stones, his queerly caved-in head. Fool that I had been never to think that Floriano himself might have smashed that head!

The bicycle had fooled me; old Mattia's own cycle,

probably, on which the murderer had been leaving, not arriving, when I had run out and stopped him. Until he had learned that I was alone, he had been afraid, having seen that open door. Having known that his crime was known.

Floriano had killed Mattia Rossi; Floriano had come to our door last night. I had understood him then, when I could not see his face.... It all made sense now. Floriano had said he had been in Volterra yesterday, when the prisoner had escaped. Of course he had! He was the escaped prisoner. Our unseen passenger, young and lithe enough to curl up in our car trunk. And, however his knowledge had been gained, he knew the villa very well indeed; he had even known where to find Roger Carstairs's diary. Because he had seen it hidden? *Or because he had hidden it himself?* He must have been very young when Roger died, but even children can kill.

But his tan—how could a prisoner in the Mastio get that tan? I was confused again, but not about one thing: I knew that he was evil....

The moon was shining into my eyes. I opened them, and saw that I was lying in a cart, upon a bed of hay. The driver's bulk loomed black above me, behind his oxen's horns. Beside it loomed another figure, taller, shapelier.

I must have moved, for he heard me and turned, white teeth flashing in that smile that now I would always hate. "You are better, carissima?"

No use pretending to be still unconscious. No use asking what he had done to Richard. To show concern for another man might be risky, an affront to his vanity. There are women who admire men who beat them; I had better pretend to be that kind. How do such women act?

I giggled nervously and sat up. "I'll feel a lot better when I've had a bath and some coffee. I must look awful." I giggled again and rubbed my jaw. "You hit hard, Floriano."

"You asked for it, carissima." He chuckled, evidently proud (as Dr. Pulcinelli had been long ago, in another world) of knowing American slang.

I made no answer; I didn't know how far to go. To overplay my act, this captivated doglike meekness—bitchy in more senses than one—might be as risky as to underplay it. His pride would prefer to think me won, but he would be watchful. Though he certainly had no reason to think me intelligent; with what disgusting ease I had swallowed all his lies!

He said nothing more, either. But the driver grinned, his own teeth flashing. He must think our quarrel over. How wrong every one of those Italian words that I had used had been! *"Aita...mio marito."* People everywhere hate to get mixed up in arguments between husband and wife. Everybody in that village must be feeling sorry for Floriano, married to a crazy foreigner. I had never had a chance.

Richard, Richard, why did I leave you? I was trying—

trying so hard—and all I did was to desert you! Leave you alone with our enemy.

For a while I simply lay there and suffered, too sick to think. The cart creaked on.

Then the driver said something in Italian, and Floriano laughed. I sat up again. The villa rose before us, huge and dark against the moon. Soon I would know!

But if Richard were still alive, God keep him unconscious! The awakening that I had longed for would be the death of him now. Floriano could not afford to leave either of us alive then. By flinging myself into his arms there in the courtyard, I had merely postponed my death. Because I was young and a woman, he would wait. And that was nothing to flatter myself about; imprisoned (in the Mastio, I supposed now), it might have been months, even years, since he had had a woman. Sickness swept over me; I lay there and shivered....

Floriano looked back over his shoulder and grinned. "We are nearly there, carissima. Soon you shall have your bath and your coffee and make yourself beautiful for me."

Again I managed that nauseating giggle.

When the cart halted before the villa, he helped me down, held me a moment, and kissed a fairly clean spot he found somewhere on my cheek. Then he let me go, abruptly.

"Truly you need that bath. I do not like my women to smell of pig."

I said meekly, "I'm sorry." I did know one thing: whatever else I might have to bear, one shame was gone forever. Never again would his touch have any power to charm the female animal in me.

As I ran past him into the villa, he turned to say good-bye to the driver. Was there an uneasy note in his laughter? To know that a whole village knows where you are cannot be pleasant for a wanted criminal, however remote and isolated that village is. Even among friends there is always, as Mattia had told Roger Carstairs long ago, one Judas. Floriano might feel that his time at the villa must be very short, now.

If he hadn't much time, then neither had we....

But all that mattered now was Richard. Richard!

Holding my breath, I ran upstairs.

Our door looked just the same; it had not been broken down. To unlock it seemed to take a long time—could my clumsiness really be unwillingness to see what was inside? Fear?

Was Richard's head lying at quite the same angle on the pillow? Blackness came over my eyes, and I swayed. I don't know how I reached him, but I did.

He was breathing! He was safe!

The blackness threatened me again, and I remembered the coffee. Floriano and I hadn't finished the last pot I had brewed. It would be cold now, but strong. I reached eagerly for my cup; but the pot was empty. Floriano must have finished it, after all. Well, I would have to face him without its help.

He was in the doorway now, smiling that everlasting smile. "Are you wondering how I got out, carissima? Without breaking down the door?"

He wanted to be admired for that too, for his cleverness in escaping. I tried to register adoring wonder. "How did you ever manage it, Floriano? Is there a secret passage?"

He laughed indulgently. "No, but to swing myself from a window onto the roof was easy. A child could do it."

"I never thought of that." I hoped I sounded properly impressed. Inwardly I was wondering what would have happened if I had had those windows wide open last night. If that lithe body had swung through....

Once more I fought off faintness, said, "Shall I make the coffee right away? You could be drinking yours while I'm in the tub." *Defer to him prettily; he will like that.*

"The sooner you are in that tub the better, carissima. I will make the coffee. I make very good coffee."

"Thank you." I hurriedly chose clean clothes, gathered them up, and headed for the bathroom. I met him coming out of it, very domestically bringing cream from the refrigerator.

He was bringing something else too: Mrs. Harris's set of kitchen knives.

I laughed; I don't know how I managed it. "Are you going to make coffee with those, Floriano?"

"You will not need them to bathe with, carissima."
Again that flash of white teeth.

I locked the bathroom door, not caring whether he heard or not. He was not going to trust me anyway. Though even if he had stood still for me to plunge it into him, I doubt if I could have done much good with a kitchen knife.

That locked door gave me a brief, exquisite illusion of safety; then once more the cold water shocked me into full consciousness. This was real; this was happening to me, Barbara Keyes, not to somebody in a book or a play. Somebody who would be saved at the last minute.

There would be no miracle for me.

For one sick minute I wondered: *Could I set my teeth and hold my head under water?* I was going to die anyway, and I might save myself a great deal of pain and humiliation.

But there was Richard. He might take out his thwarted fury on Richard.

I toweled myself savagely, I almost poured on perfume. If I put on too much for Floriano's taste, good; he might send me back to scrub some of it off. I would gain a little time, if only a very little.

I combed my hair, painted my face, and put on a smile. Also my new coral chiffon; I remembered with almost unbearable misery how proud and happy I had been the one time I had worn it before. For Richard. But if there was even a thousandth chance that I could beguile Floriano, get him off guard—

He whistled at sight of me. *"Bellissima!"*

I said again, rather idiotically, "Thank you."

He was entirely the gentleman now, loverly but well-bred. When I praised his coffee extravagantly, he was obliging enough to brew another pot, but I could manage no further delay. The time came, dreadfully soon, when I had to push back my chair and rise.

"I'd better tidy up now, Floriano."

"No." He rose too, laughing. "You are a good little housewife. And that is well, but I know what will be better. Come."

There was coffee in the pot this time. Hot coffee. I could throw it in his face. With luck could blind him—

No. I might be able to escape him then, but Richard couldn't. Blind, he could still find the bed....

He was lighting the lantern I had bought in Volterra. Above its glowing paleness, his eyes laughed and sparkled, very black.

"We will go to my room, carissima. My own place, the room I had here as a boy. All my boyhood treasures are still there, all the clothes I had when first I became a young man. This suit I am wearing came from there. You did not know that I grew up in the Villa Carenni, did you? My windows too look out upon the garden. There will be moonlight."

"Why do you want that lantern?" I didn't really care; but even a question takes time.

"The better to see you by. The moonlight may not

be enough, and electric light is too harsh to fall upon a beautiful woman's flesh."

As we went out into the dark corridor together, his arm closed round me, held me close. I was not going to get the chance to break away and run.

We made a turn, went into the east wing, which I had thought the original guest quarters. At its far end was a walled staircase, black as the pit. Perhaps twenty feet from it was a door that Floriano opened. I caught one glimpse of the room within, no servant's room, but wide and spacious, moonlight pouring through long windows onto the fantastic, richly carved furniture. Then I gasped and caught his arm, making the lantern shake. "Floriano! What was that?"

His free hand shot out, holding the lantern farther from me. "What is what? I saw nothing."

"Over there, by the stairs! Something moved!"

Let him believe me—let him! Let his grasp loosen for just one second, then I could dash the lantern from his hand and flee into the darkness. He would follow me, not turn back to hurt Richard, and these stone floors and walls could not catch fire. It was not much of a chance, but it was my last.

But Floriano's hold did not loosen. He sat the lantern down just inside the door, out of my reach. His mouth still smiled, but his eyes were hard.

"Still playing tricks, carissima? This one is old, very old. I do not like to be bored." His voice was silken-soft, but something in it made me shiver.

"I'm not. It may be Mattia Rossi's murderer—"

"That one?" His smile broadened. "He will not come, my pretty; I can promise you that. We are quite alone—"

"Not quite, my son."

The cold, cultured voice was not loud, but it rang through the dark hall like a bell. It had the smooth hardness of a bell.

I felt the start that made Floriano's whole body jerk. He stared, as I stared, towards the stairs. Into the blackness that seemed to be opening and giving birth....

We could not see the tall man who advanced upon us as anything but blackness, moving, towering darkness. Shadow, terribly made substance. He stopped just before the lantern light could reach him, make him human.

Yet Floriano knew him. He cowered; his voice rose in a thin wailing whisper, *"Tu! tu!* (You! You!)"

The gun rang out, thunder-loud in that narrow space, between those stone walls. With a crash that seemed as if it must end the world.

CHAPTER VIII

Floriano screamed once. He still stood erect, and for a second I thought, "He hasn't been shot after all." Then I saw how his right arm hung.

The newcomer's voice came again, velvet-soft now. With something terrifying in its very calm. "It will not be necessary to watch you quite so carefully now, my son. Disablement will curb those animal spirits of yours."

Floriano moaned something that might have been either a prayer or a curse. The voice reproved him. "A communist calling upon God, my son? I never taught you such Christian superstitions as prayer, and you know better than to use profanity before a lady. Speak her own tongue, and such words as are fit for her to hear. You were taught languages, also your manners.... Your pardon, signora." He turned to me and bowed with courtly grace. "Allow me to present myself:

Prince Mino Carenni. Under happier circumstances, your host."

"You are alive!" Floriano shrank back, staring at him as a hypnotized bird is said to stare at a snake, but obediently he spoke English now. "How can you be alive? How?"

"I never died, my son. But I will explain later, satisfy this most touching filial concern of yours. First, let all of us go into your room. You too, signora."

I went, wondering if I were dreaming. I couldn't have raised Prince Mino's ghost, it couldn't have shot Floriano. And it couldn't be Floriano's father.

"...please obey me, signora. Be so kind as to search our dear one's pockets. He probably carries weapons."

He had been speaking again, speaking to me, and I hadn't heard. I jumped, said, "I'm sorry," and obeyed hastily. I found an ugly-looking knife. With another bow he took it from me.

"This only, my son? No pistol?"

"Not a gun in the gun room is loaded! You know that; you must have hidden the ammunition. Or else this woman did." Floriano flashed me a glance of pure hate.

"Do not speak rudely to the lady, my son. It was the good Signora Harris, not she or I, who made poor Mattia remove the ammunition. She is of those ladies who fear firearms.... But we neglect your wound." Again he swung to me. "In that chest of drawers yonder, you will find shirts and handkerchiefs, signora."

I was still dazed. I didn't move at once and he said, with his first touch of impatience, "Would you let him bleed to death? You who a moment ago were his lover?"

"That isn't true." Indignation should have helped me, but it didn't. My voice shook as I tried to explain. "My husband is here, hurt. Unconscious. I tried to go for help, but this man stopped me. I couldn't get away from him."

"A moment ago you were making no great effort to escape." The fine old voice was dry. "But your love affairs are no concern of mine, signora. Be pleased to help him off with his jacket and to bandage him; also be careful not to stand between him and me while you do so. You will not need to bathe or disinfect the wound. Stand still, my son! I do not wish to shoot you again."

Why was no disinfectant needed? My hands were cold as I rather clumsily did Prince Mino's bidding.

"Enough. That is well." He swung away the lantern, whose light he had been directing upon Floriano's bleeding flesh. He set it down, and I had my first good look at him. At a tall lean man with white hair and piercing black eyes. His profile, stern and finely chiseled, might have been cut out of an ancient frieze; it had none of the softness of living flesh.

He glanced around the big, pleasant room. "All here is just as you left it, my son. Old Mattia kept it carefully; he always hoped for your return. Almost as much as I did, though for different reasons. He never would believe that you had meant to betray me."

"You touch me." Floriano's lip curled.

Prince Mino ignored him, spoke to me. "There was a time when I took pride in this young man, signora." Neither his eyes nor the hand that held the pistol wavered, but his voice had grown thoughtful, almost wistful. "As a boy he showed great promise. He had beauty, and what is better, sensitiveness to beauty. He had charm and gaiety; he brought laughter between these old walls that have heard too little laughter. Even when I began to realize his limitations, I did not fully understand that he had greed, not ambition, vanity, not pride, a certain facile cleverness but no true intelligence—"

"Did I need all those fine things?" Floriano's voice was harsh. "I am a bastard. I never could have been a Prince Carenni."

"You could have been many things. A scholar and a gentleman among them. A rich man, too—and wealth you do value. You were not bred like a bastard."

"Although my mother was brought here to serve as maid to the principessa? To your fine lady wife? Before whom we could never speak to you save as to our master? To spare her feelings—as if she did not know the truth as well as we three knew it!" Floriano spat.

"She was a noble lady who understood her obligations, the duties of her position. A gentleman also has obligations, as I tried to teach you. When you could not learn them, I realized that our house could not be reborn through you." The fine old voice was unruffled, but it sounded weary. "You have thrown away a great deal that you might have had."

"You say so now. But would you ever have given me enough to matter? You were tiring of me—withdrawing from me—"

"All that you could have understood, I would have given to you. For I was still foolishly proud of you, of your beauty and grace and strength. I never dreamed that you lacked even the simple virtue of a dog: loyalty."

"Were you entitled to my loyalty?" Again, Floriano spat.

"I was. And for that lack I will exact the penalty." The quiet, metal-hard voice had not risen, but its coldness made me shiver. "Sit down—there, on that chair; rest a little. We have a long way to go, and I do not wish you to faint before we reach our destination. But first place a chair for the lady. I regret that you must accompany us, signora."

"Where?" My lips framed the word, but no sound came. I sat down, and Floriano sat down. Without taking his eyes from us, the prince drew up another chair.

"While we wait we may talk. You wondered how I came to be alive, my son. That is simple. I wished to return to my own house, to my work. The latter must be finished before I die. Though doubtless neither of you can comprehend that necessity." The cool scorn in those old eyes flicked at both of us like a whip.

"He let you go! Dr. Manelli! He couldn't have been such a fool!" Floriano spoke savagely.

"He owed the Carenni much; my father paid for the medical schooling of his. Also"—a faint smile flickered over the princely mouth—"during the war he had found it prudent, though never pleasant, to oblige the Nazis in certain small ways. Many men did as much, but he came to fear that my lawyers held papers that might convict him of collaboration."

"You blackmailed him." Floriano laughed shortly.

"I had no need to threaten the good Dr. Manelli, my son. He became very grateful for my kindness in suppressing the documents."

"What was the difference?" A shrill note had come into Floriano's laughter. "Your delicate reminders—"

"A very great one, my son, though too subtle, perhaps, for peasant wits to appreciate. Fear is the basis of all authority; it is necessary to keep a whip in a drawer, yet distasteful to bring it out."

"Do you find cruelty so distasteful, signore?" A sneer twisted Floriano's beautiful mouth.

"It is without beauty, my son. Until one has learned to hate greatly…. Be so good as not to interrupt me. The urn that was sent here contains ashes, though not mine. It came by day, I by night. Poor old Mattia took me for a ghost at first—I was sorry to give the old fellow such a fright."

For a second he paused, and I found courage to speak. "But whose ashes were they? Surely this Dr. Manelli didn't kill somebody for you!"

He looked amused. "No, signora. He had an old gardener whose family had died in the war, a man for whom few inquiries would be made. He listed this fellow's heart ailment on my chart, he gave him a small room in the sanitarium grounds, and when he died, the man who took him away for cremation thought that they carried my body. Nothing about the death certificate was irregular save the substitution of my name for his. So I was free to return here. To come home, as you would say."

"And it needed no threat to make Mattia risk himself for you—that good, stupid dog!" Floriano snarled.

"He was loyal, my son. The thing that you can never understand." Suddenly the old voice was unmistakably weary.

"And you let him sell some of those gold Etruscan things to pay for food and whatever else you needed! You, who never would let me touch even the least of them!" There was fury in Floriano's voice.

"Because you cared only for the gold, my son. Not for its beauty or its workmanship." The tired voice was bitter. "But he sold little; for many years my needs have been simple."

"It wasn't Mattia Rossi who accused you to the Allies, was it?" I was surprised to hear myself asking that.

"That honest old servant?" Prince Mino stiffened, with the first simple human anger I had seen him show. "Never. So you had to blacken his name, my son? His death was not enough?"

"I didn't mean to kill him; I didn't want to!" Floriano's protesting hands flew wide, then the pain in his shoulder made him gasp. "He tried to frighten me—to make me leave. And he did lie to me—he said that you were coming, not that you were here. I didn't believe him, I did not think you could be alive, but I saw that I could not trust him—him that I had been so sure would help me—" His voice broke in a sob of self-pity.

Prince Mino smiled thinly. "He thought to save us from each other. You were always his great weakness, you who had tagged at his heels as a little one. And he has paid dearly for it. You, whom he loved, murdered him. As you murdered Roger Carstairs."

I gasped. Floriano laughed again, wildly, in hysterical triumph.

"Yes, I killed them, I killed them both! I've blackened your precious name, I've driven you into hiding! With my peasant's wit I've made you—you, the great noble Prince Carenni—a fugitive skulking in your own cellars. Dependent on a servant you held no higher than a faithful dog! And now I've taken even him from you. I've finished you! If you stay here, you'll starve. Whatever you do to me, I've done that to you! I!"

"It needn't be that way." I spoke eagerly. "You have

me for a witness, Prince Mino. You've done nothing. You can live in your own house again, openly, your name cleared."

He smiled with good-humored contempt. "You— would you be likely to bear witness against your lover?"

"He is not my lover!"

"Then appearances were most deceiving when first I came upon the two of you, signora." His smile deepened.

Floriano smiled too, impishly. "You hurt me, carissima. I had thought we loved with great passion—"

"Be silent." Prince Mino lifted an imperious hand. "And you, signora, I sincerely regret your involvement in this matter. But it cannot be helped now."

Under those terrible, passionless eyes, I shrank and was silent. They swung back to Floriano. "Why did you murder my guest, my son? You did not know him; he had nothing you could have wanted."

"You talked to him; you showed him things!" Floriano was almost shouting now. "Things you never showed me! I knew that; I listened, listened at the door. Many times. I knew he was in the villa before you did. I saw Mattia find him. Even Mattia befriended him, hid him from me!"

"Sneaking and spying were born in you." The prince's voice and eyes were equally hard, equally cold. "Vanity and jealousy also; but you did not kill for these."

"He meant to steal the treasure!" Floriano's voice rose even higher. "He deceived you; he searched for it. Perhaps Mattia helped him! He found it; he was writing about that in his diary when I came in behind him. I had thought he would be asleep, I had drugged his drink, but he was not! He looked up—"

"And you killed him. Out of fear." Prince Mino's eyes were grim indeed now. "Gold was not what he sought, but that you could never understand. He should have stayed in his room, as I bade him, but in a young man so closely imprisoned, folly was inevitable. He too came of inferior stock."

"He was looking for gold! Any man with a brain looks for gold!"

"Any man with your kind of brain." Again Prince Mino's voice cut like a whip. "You murdered your father's guest, and then, when the Allied officers came with their questions, you panicked and planted evidence against me, your father. Is that not so?"

Sweat stood on Floriano's face, his throat worked.

"Answer me. Is that not so?"

"I was afraid that Mattia would tell you. He had seen me coming up out of the cellars." Floriano groaned.

"So? Then Mattia was fortunate to live as long as he did. But he suspected you only of spying, not murder."

"He loved me better than you ever did!"

"Longer, at least.... You changed your name for fear of me, an imprisoned old man. But I had my watchers. I knew when you joined the communists—those mad, murderous vermin who are yet too good for such as you, since they do not set gold above all else."

"They kill princes. They do not hold bastardy against a man! They are the hope of the world." All Floriano's old fanaticism flamed up, though his eyes, fixed upon his father's, still made me think of a bird's transfixed by a snake.

"A great hope, truly. They taught you to roast poor old Giovanni Quilico alive in his own furnace. And a weakling government only sent you to the Mastio."

I jumped. This must have been the outrage that Dr. Pulcinelli had spoken of, and I, like a fool, had thought Floriano too fine, too fastidious, to have had any part in it.

"Yet the most doting father could not have rejoiced more than I when I heard of your escape, my son. Or have sorrowed more sincerely when he heard of your recapture." Prince Mino's voice was colder, more biting that the bitterest wind. "For had you had to serve your full sentence before you returned—as I knew well that you would return, faithful to your vulgar dreams of buried gold!—I might have been too old and too feeble to give you the welcome due you, my son."

Floriano swallowed, but made no sound. He still stared at his father, bird facing snake. And Prince Mino suddenly seemed to tire of the game. He rose. "You have rested long enough. It is time to go. Be so good as to pick up the lantern, signora."

I had expected that. I had known it must be coming, but when I picked up the lantern, my hand shook so that the prince reached out and steadied it. He looked at it appraisingly. "This does not belong here. But it is well made."

I said shakily, glad of anything to gain a moment's time, "I bought it in Volterra yesterday. Taddeo Credi made it."

Then I shivered, remembering my feeling when I had left Taddeo's workshop, the unseen eyes watching me, the footsteps following me. I had been right. Death had followed me back to the Palazzo Verocchio, death masquerading as youth and beauty. Floriano, escaping a second time. His first escape must have lasted long enough to rid him of his prison pallor, give him the tan that had fooled me....

Prince Mino's voice called me back. "I am glad to see that the old fellow has not lost his touch." He was still looking at the lantern.

"He should have cut your heart out with his chisel long ago!" Floriano's voice was savage; something had suddenly brought back his courage. "Many a peasant has killed his daughter's seducer. But he did not. He hoped that you would make him rich. He licked your boots."

"Your grandfather is a sensible man. I set him up in his own shop in Volterra. He knew that he did not have it in him to rise higher." Prince Mino's voice was calm, unruffled. It was I who started. Then Rossana Credi—the beautiful Rossana—

"And my mother? How high did you raise her?" Floriano's eyes were burning.

"I gave Rossana what to her was luxury. If she had not been too foolish to behave herself, she might still be enjoying it." Prince Mino's voice was still unruffled.

"Yes, she was foolish!"

Floriano's voice stabbed like a knife. "A woman needs more than luxury, more than old withered flesh, even if it is princely flesh. A prince—bah! She was young and beautiful. She saw a young man, and he saw her. She gave herself, she who had been sold before. How you made him run away, I do not know, but what you did to her I know!"

"What exactly do you know?" Prince Mino's face had suddenly become very still.

"You terrified her first; you made her feel cheap, ashamed. A faithless harlot, you called her—you who had taken her for your pleasure. If ever she was a harlot, you made her one." Floriano's voice shook.

"Even then you were an eavesdropper, my son?" Prince Mino's face still had that inhuman stillness.

"They who have a master learn such tricks early." Floriano's voice stabbed at him again. "I was little, but I remember. I heard your voice; I can still hear her weeping." He paused; the room itself seemed suddenly very still. Nothing in it moved, nothing but the shadows that flickered beyond the lantern light.

"We thought you sent her away to serve in the house of friends of yours in Florence, people who would watch her well and see if she mended her ways. We hoped that in time you would let her come back, my grandparents and I. My grandmother burned many candles before the Virgin." Floriano's voice shook. "And then you told us that she was dead."

"Only you believed that. I told your grandfather that she had gone away with a new lover." Prince Mino's voice was as expressionless as his face.

"I see. So you made sure that they would never seek her grave. Even a rabbit like Taddeo Credi must have killed you had he known the truth!"

"Which you found out?" Still that serene, deadly voice.

"I heard the address you gave your chauffeur when you sent her away. The street number I forgot, but the name of the street I always remembered." Floriano's voice shook. "Later, in my teens, I found among your papers an address on that street. And next time you took me into Florence—and left me to amuse myself while you went off with your fine friends that I was not good enough to meet!—I went to look at that house to which you had sent my mother. It was not the kind of street I expected, not the kind of house I expected. Yet still I did not understand until I knocked on the door and they let me in!

"That was folly." Into the taut hush Prince Mino's tones fell, cool, undisturbed. "Older men than you have picked up evil sicknesses in that place."

"I was not green, my noble father. I drank with the girl they gave me, but I did not touch her. I paid her for the name of an old woman who worked there. No inmate—inmates of a place like that do not live to be old. But that old hag who scrubbed floors remembered a very pretty girl called Rossana, one who must have come there at about the right date. One who died soon. That was all I could be glad of—that she died soon!" He shuddered, then turned blazing eyes upon his father. "How much did they pay you for my mother, most noble father? Or were you too proud to take money from such as they? Did you give her to them as a free gift—the mother of your son?"

The silence that fell then cannot have lasted very long, but it was very deep.

"It was not well done." Prince Mino spoke as if to himself. "I have since regretted such outraging of beauty.... Treachery came to you with her blood, but there was no malice in her, only weakness. She did not earn her fate, as you have earned yours."

He shrugged again, as if shaking off some slight, clinging encumbrance. "We must go now. You first, signora. For now I will carry the lantern."

Courteously he stood aside for me to precede him through the door. Like automatons Floriano and I moved at his bidding. It was as if we were machines, and he had pressed the buttons that controlled us. Floriano's defiance was over, spent with the fury that he had hurled at the icy, impregnable fortress of his father's pride. He was in pain, but that did not matter, even to him, except because his disablement kept him from fighting for his life.

It had been meant to do just that. Prince Mino easily could have planted that bullet in his son's heart, but he had not. Why?

Not because of pity. Not because of scruples....

I remembered Burckhardt's great work on Renaissance Italy, his description of the *bella vendetta*, that "beautiful vengeance" that must be a work of art, something worth years of waiting and planning. An agony that tore soul as well as body, and the cooler, the more dispassionate its infliction, the more the avenger had been admired. My skin crawled.

Floriano stumbled against the wall and groaned. Pain has a terrible anonymity; it wipes out personality. I put out my hand to help him, as I would have anybody else; then met Prince Mino's eyes and knew that I had made another mistake. He knew very little about pity; if he had had any doubt that I was his son's lover, he was satisfied now.

"Let him be, signora. Go on." The implacable, polished voice did not rise, but I went on.

We came into the kitchen; our captor herded us toward the cellar door.

We were going down into the vaults!

Realizing that, I woke up, lost the queer feeling of moving will-less through a dream. I stopped and faced my enemy. "Please, Prince Mino—whatever you think of me, my husband has never harmed you. He's here in your house, hurt—"

"You wish to go back to care for him? Most touching

wifely solicitude, signora, but you will soon forget it again. As you forgot it before, in my son's arms." Again his dry smile cut like a whip.

But this time a kind of queer, cold courage came to me. I said, "You want to believe that. To play the righteous judge, miles above Floriano and me. But you can't stay up those glorious heights if you let my husband die. Then you'll be a common criminal, just as Floriano is. Just another murderer."

He was silent a moment; then he said, "I have always meant to see that help came to your husband, signora. It will; that much I promise you."

I said, "Thank you," and I meant it. But Floriano burst into wild laughter. "You fool! Can't you see that he means to kill you too?"

I said, "I know that."

I suppose I had known it all along, but saying it gave me a strange, freezing feeling of finality; and both men looked at me in surprise. There was even a touch of respect in the prince's voice as he said, "I am sorry, signora; I regret the necessity. But I must have a little more time; my work must be finished. And that work is too important to be risked for the sake of an adulteress."

I didn't try to answer him; it didn't seem to be worthwhile. And when the cellar door swung open, the light itself seemed to shiver and recoil from the darkness below.

CHAPTER IX

It is a strange thing to look down into darkness—utter, abyss-like darkness—and to know that you are going to go down into it, and will never come up again. Prince Mino's voice seemed to come from very far away. "Be pleased to descend, signora."

And I did exactly that. Dumb, docile as sheep, Floriano and I moved before him. It is terrible, the human instinct to obey; the secret that Madame Montessori and Mussolini—those two very different Italians—both knew. Perhaps it gives hypnotists their power too.

My heels rang upon those stones on which I had seen old Mattia Rossi lying in his blood. Those stones from which he had been dragged to his unknown grave.

Soon now Floriano and I would find our graves....

Well, for Floriano that was fair enough; he had

smashed that bloodstained gray head. But what had I done? Anger flooded me, stiffened me. What right had Prince Mino to judge me? Why had I let him cow me? I shouldn't have wasted those few minutes on the stairs; I could have jumped past Floriano, have knocked—at least have tried to knock—my lantern from the prince's hand.

As if in answer, his voice came: "Please take the lantern now, signora. Also remember that from now on my flashlight will be in my left hand, as my pistol is in my right. Any trickery will only compel me to act at once."

He set the lantern down; I picked it up.

We went on. We came to another staircase. The stale smell of the depths came up to us, closed round us. I thought dreamily, unbelievingly, "I shall never breathe fresh air again."

That didn't seem real. Nothing did.

Passage followed passage; chamber after chamber opened off them. We were below the cellars now, among the tombs. The painted walls swarmed with a myriad forms; sometimes demons glared at us, sometimes dancers rioted along beside us, men red as American Indians clasping milk-white women. One could almost see their delight in their bodies, in their leaping, spinning, amorous strength, although those bodies were only paint on stone. Crazily I wished that I could jump onto the wall too, and dance away with them, happy and safe. Then, looking a little closer at some of those fiercely joyous red faces, I knew that I couldn't have said "No" to those men as long as I had said it to Floriano. They would simply have grabbed me.

Floriano. From time to time I saw his face, drawn with pain, slack with despair. Fear was older in him than rebellion; he was conquered. But I had not obeyed Prince Mino from childhood; deep down under the dream, something at the core of me waited, angry and watchful.

We went on and on, down, down.

The lantern was getting very heavy. For a long time the air had been bad, and it was getting worse. My lungs sucked at its lifeless weight. We must be in the very bowels of the Earth now; only this wasn't Earth. These walls that pressed in upon us had been hewn out of the rock that lies beneath our planet's life-giving pad of soil; they were further down than life should go. We were indeed in the Underworld, in the very Kingdom of the Dead....

"Only a little farther now, signora." That courteous voice of Prince Mino's! "We are near that sanctuary in which, until I discovered it in 1939, no man had set foot for over two thousand years."

The place Roger Carstairs had found! For the first time in what seemed hours, I remembered the diary.

Floriano's face glowed. The beauty that had faded from it flashed back, like the lighting of a lamp. "The treasure chamber! You are taking us to it!"

"I am. It seems fitting, my son, that you should see that for which you have taken two men's lives. For which soon you will give your own life."

The light went out of Floriano's face; his shoulders sagged. But my heart leapt with a wild gladness. Time! This should give us a little more time!

We came to a place where two huge slabs of stone rose starkly, massive double doors guarded by two more of the squat urn-men, with their weirdly lifelike red faces.

"These should not be here." Prince Mino sounded almost apologetic. "My ancestor took them from their proper places. It was some whim of his to set them to guard what he had placed within."

Which ancestor—and what had he placed within? *Dear God, don't let it be what I'm thinking of.* My courage was gone again; I was remembering what I least wanted to remember.

"Open the doors, my son."

Those stone slabs would have been heavy for a man with two good arms, a man who had lost no blood. Sweat ran down Floriano's face; his big black eyes looked like a suffering child's. *He is a child*, I thought suddenly. *Too locked up in himself, in his own desires and grievances, to realize that anyone else has any rights, even the right to live.* I had very little reality for him, my feelings and motives none. Childish spite would keep him from ever speaking the words that might clear me.

But if he had spoken, would Prince Mino have

believed him? Could he have afforded to? I had to be expendable.

At last the doors opened. Again I was given precedence. That too is a queer feeling—to go through a door and know that you may never come out again.

Before us stretched another passageway, perhaps twenty feet long. At its end was a vast circular chamber. Burial niches lined its walls, stone beds divided from one another by the rock walls out of which they had been hewn. *They look exactly like railroad berths*, I thought, and nearly started laughing again.

A gigantic central pillar supported the ceiling. It had been cracked across, and fresh mortar-work showed like bandages on a wound. Prince Mino surveyed it, frowning.

"Some years ago an Earth tremor weakened this pillar. Yesterday it began to crumble in places. Had poor Mattia not been down here helping me to repair it, he would have been on hand to greet you and your husband, signora. Much might have gone otherwise."

I felt sick. On his way up from here, old Mattia must have met Floriano. If he had not—if he had not—my legs trembled; the prince looked at me with concern.

"You are faint, signora? Seat yourself there on that sarcophagus behind you. Stand beside her, my son."

I sat down—flopped down, rather—on the edge of one of those quaint stone berths. Prince Mino walked towards another, swung the flashlight into its shadows, and reached down. When he straightened I saw something dangle, gleaming, from his hand.

A pair of handcuffs!

I screamed then; at least I tried to. All I heard was the kind of feeble squeak you make in nightmares. I knew, then, what it was that I had been afraid of all along.

To lie in one of these stone beds forever. Until my bones crumbled, like those of that girl for whom the villa had been made beautiful long ago. Only I would lie beside Floriano.

"No! No!" Floriano cowered back, his eyes seeming to start from his head. "No!" He must have feared what I feared.

"No unseemly exhibitions, my son," the prince reproved him coldly. "These toys will not hurt you. They should fit you well, having once held the famous murderess Orsini, she who poisoned not only her husband, but her child. Her own blood, one as close to her as a father.... Your pardon, signora."

I felt something cold close round my wrist, heard something snap. I looked down and saw the handcuff gleaming there. Its mate gleamed around Floriano's wrist. We too were linked together, inescapably. Prince Mino said calmly, "Your grandfather had a taste for such gauds, my son. You may remember his collections. Of late years I brought these down here, in case of uninvited intruders, and now they serve me well."

He turned his back on us, moved to yet another of those stone berths. For an awful instant I thought he meant it to be our deathbed. I could almost hear him say, "Come here. Lie down." But then I saw that he was looking at the wall that divided that berth from the one just left of it. The fronts of all those dividers looked like separate panels, set into the living rock of which they actually were parts, so carefully had they been carved to resemble wood. Prince Mino seemed to play with those carvings, fingering them like a child. I thought, *Has he gone completely mad?*

Then wondered if I had, for suddenly what had seemed to be solid rock swung outwards. The panel was a door, several inches deep; its carved border had disguised the edges. The black cavity behind it did not look a full eighteen inches wide, but it was there!

Floriano and I both gasped. His father swung to face us, shining-eyed. "This is the entrance to the shrine of Mania, Goddess of the Abyss. Its priests buried themselves and it beneath a planned avalanche, to keep out Sulla's butchers. So they saved their holy place from such rape as the Temple of Veltha suffered."

He paused, actually smiling at us. For the first time we had some value to him, not as ourselves, but as an audience. And I could have smiled back; my heart felt as if all the rock around us had just been rolled off it. For now, at least, our handcuffs were only restraints, meant to give him full freedom of action.

Nothing else....

His eyes shone, his face was rapt. "Later, under the empire, the family of Tequna, descendants of those old priestly guardians, had this room dug out and made it their family tomb. Giving their dead bodies to guard their holy place even as that earlier head of their house—the last of the high priests—have given his living body. When I found this door, I swore that the trust they had kept through the ages never should be betrayed through me."

And it won't be, I thought sickeningly, *because what Floriano and I see won't matter. We're going to die.*

"You are ready, signora? I regret to say that at first you must walk sidewise, and always downward. Also we must leave your lovely lantern behind." With that maddening courtesy, the straight old figure moved to one side, cool again, a gracious host.

That black slit yawned before us. Floriano and I entered it, groped a little way, then heard the door close and panicked. Stone scraped our shoulders, we writhed against each other like snakes, pocketed in blinding, terrifying blackness. When I heard Prince Mino's voice behind us, I could have sobbed with relief. "A few more yards, and the way will widen."

Those few yards seemed terribly long. It was wonderful when Floriano and I finally had room enough to walk side by side. The rock walls pressing in upon us made the ghastly tomb chamber we had just left seem like freedom, like the sunlit outside world. Prince Mino kept well behind us; his flashlight gave us just enough light to watch our footing.

I don't know how long we walked; I do know that

every step led downward. The passage kept twisting, turning, until I thought, *This is what it would feel like if one had been swallowed by a snake.* I even began to imagine that I could hear the creature hissing.

It was getting warmer, too. If I had been hurt, like Floriano, I should have thought that I had fever. And the hissing was getting louder, fiercer, filling my whole head. I could smell some kind of odor.

"Steady." That was Prince Mino's voice again, closer behind us now. "Soon we shall be there, signora."

Where? I wondered. *In Hell?* We did seem to have gone far enough down to get there.

We made one last turn, and then suddenly I could feel the blackness widening, opening, like an awful flower. There was still that odor, but I could breathe again. Though, oddly, the hissing seemed louder.

"Careful. Here the ramp ends and the stairs begin." Prince Mino swung the flashlight forward.

Space swam before us, immense black space from which that hissing rose, sinister, sibilant, as if rising from the throats of a myriad serpents, writhing in the depths below.

Floriano let out a yell. *"Madre di dio!"*

He whirled, sprang at his father. The cold face did not change, but the hand that held the pistol swung, snake-swift, with scientific precision. Floriano yelled again and reeled back, a bloody gash across his temple.

"I have told you to speak English. Control yourself. You have only one thing to fear here: me."

That last probably was true enough, I thought, struggling to regain my balance. Floriano's lunge had nearly jerked me off my feet.

"Again I apologize for my son, signora. There is no cause for alarm. See." He raised the flashlight again. We had come out of the passage, stood upon a kind of landing. I saw a wide stone staircase leading down into a huge cavern. White, hissing steam veiled one end. I looked and understood.

"Gas! Natural gas. Like the pillars Richard says they have at Larderello."

"Yes. This is a land of underground fires. Can you wonder, signora, that when the early Rasenna found this cave and the abyss within it—for it is an abyss from which this curtain of steam rises—they took it for an entrance to the Underworld? A shrine built by Mania herself to herself?"

"There are snakes! I saw them!" Floriano's eyes were dazed, but still wild, suspicious. "Down there."

He pointed, and Prince Mino's lip curled. "True. Yet I hardly think they will bite you, my son."

He tilted the flashlight, and we saw the far side of the cavern. A building round as a ring stood there, the strangest, most fantastic building I have ever seen. Monstrous figures, red, black, blue, and purple, swarmed over it, reared angrily from its roof. But in the center of that roof, high above them all, stood the gigantic figure of a woman crowned with snakes.

No wonder that Floriano, catching just a glimpse

of those snakes in the torch rays, had thought them alive. They seemed to hiss and curl, a crown of living death. The face below had an awful beauty, not base, not vicious, majestic, perhaps even noble, but infinitely remote from the heat of all passion, from all the softening gentleness of pity. She stared with unwinking black eyes into that hissing curtain of steam that could never warm her. Whether those eyes were made of obsidian or some other shiny black stone I don't know, but they looked alive.

One long, exquisite hand, thrice the size of any mortal woman's, hung at her side. The other held a staff upon which perched a dove. That winged symbol united her with Heaven and the immensities of space, even as the serpent crown allied her with the crawling things of the depths.

"Eos." I said it aloud. "Eos." But no, that misnamed dawn goddess in the garden far above us was only a shadow of this. Of the goddess behind all goddesses, "One from with many names," the creatress who created all only to feed death. Life seemed shrunken to a thing made only that one might suffer the agony of giving it up. Since I could not turn my eyes away, I closed them.

"Mania, Queen of the Dead and of the Underworld." Prince Mino's voice held something like reverence, the last quality I ever had expected to hear in it. "Mother and murderess. From that broad breast all life sprang, and to it all life must return."

"She can't be a mother! She couldn't be!" My voice

broke; in some dreadful way that I could not explain, even to myself, I knew that she could be.

"Our beginning and our end. The queen to whom we must all bow at last. So the ancient Rasenna saw her, and when one by one their Twelve Cities fell and they knew that they had no empire left save in her, the Unconquerable, they brought their greatest treasures here, to her keeping."

"The treasure!" Incredibly, the eagerness was back in Floriano's voice. He leapt forward, but once more his father's voice stopped him. "Not so fast, my son. You do not wish the lady to fall."

Floriano did not care whether I fell or not, and several times on those stairs I thought we both would. When we reached the cavern floor he ran forward, half-dragging me. He seemed to have forgotten his pain and weakness. Even his father, following us like a grim shepherd.

I heard his voice behind us, fast in his own dream: "Through generation after generation those galleries above us were hewn and widened, turned into tombs. Pilgrims from all Twelve Cities sought burial here."

"Paying high for the privilege, no doubt. Priests always have been greedy liars." Floriano found breath enough to sneer.

"For rest under the mother's own wings? To them it was worth the price, my son. But gold could not buy entrance into this holy of holies. It was opened but once a year, and then only those might enter whom the goddess had summoned in a dream. It was so with other ancient sanctuaries of the chthonian Powers, but seldom, surely, with so much cause as here."

"But those dream-summoned fools brought gold to pay for their she-devil's favor!" Floriano's laugh was evil.

"Don't call her that. Not here." I don't know why I spoke. We had almost reached the temple now. She was towering above us, very near, the curtain of mist behind her now. It seemed to cling to her great arms, to fall from them, like vast, gauzy wings. Give her power to swoop and seize, like Eos—

"We have arrived. I have a lamp inside. When I have lit it, I will call you." Prince Mino stepped across the threshold, and we waited, Floriano licking his lips, his hands clenching and unclenching.

Then light streamed from the doorway, Prince Mino called "Enter," and we rushed in. Or Floriano did, nearly upsetting me.

I gasped, thinking we were in the midst of a whole crowd of people. Then I saw that they were statues, and every one of them a masterpiece. Statues of bronze and terra cotta, of men and women; there was even one of a child, his hair all shining silver; Tages, I supposed. Some had faces and bodies of terrible power; others were laughing, delighting with fierce exuberance in their own youth and beauty. It was hard to believe that they were not alive. Whenever I looked away from one, the shining black obsidian eyes of the others seemed to follow me. There may have been coffers at their feet, jewels on some of them; I don't know. They were overwhelming, and a little nervously I looked away from them, at the painted walls that had been built higher than most Etruscan walls, to support that mighty Figure on the roof.

There was nothing evil; all must have dated back to the days when the Twelve Cities of the Rasenna were still young and happy. Horses galloped along those ring-round walls, through fields of brilliant poppies. Birds flew above them. From the rear wall, Mania herself looked down, with the same noble, aweing face that the statue wore above, but here the promise of eternal life was in it, the warm beauty of the Earth Mother in whose brown breast the seed is buried, only to rise again. I forgot that I was under sentence of death; I only wished that Richard were here too, to enjoy all this.

"The gold!" Floriano demanded hotly, impatiently. "Where is the gold?" He had found his voice again. I think that for a little while all those shining, watching obsidian eyes must have daunted him.

"Be patient, my son; you shall see the treasure. But this room should interest you in other ways. Here Mattia and I laid Roger Carstairs's body for a little while. Poor old Mattia never could rid himself of his peasant superstitions; he wished to say a prayer over the corpse before we consigned it to the abyss, and I humored him. I said no prayer, but my heart was heavy last night when I carried him down into these depths.

He always shrank from them, endured them only for my sake. He would have wanted a grave beneath the sun."

"You brought him down here?" Floriano looked startled. "You actually bent your noble back to carry your good dog to his last resting place? He was good, in his fool's way. I wish it had been you I met in the cellars! Killing you would have been a joy that I would have remembered gladly all the days of my life, no matter how long I lived."

"Almost we met," his father said dryly. "I came in time to see you running upstairs. Fleeing from a dead man, with that cowardice you got from the Credis. I was unarmed then, or your death might have been quick. Which would have been a pity. It will not be, now."

I heard the quick indrawing of Floriano's breath, felt myself shiver. Yet to have carried Mattia Rossi's body down here must have been a terrible task for an old man. Had some quirk of the sentiment he despised moved him, kept him from letting his old servant's body lie untended on the stones? Or had he feared discovery, a real search of the vaults? It might be important to know, though I could not imagine much gentleness in him.

I said, "You brought Roger's body down here— cremated it in a way—so that there would be no evidence?"

"You might put it so. Then Mattia and I did the work that was not undone until after my return two months ago. A small explosion that crumbled walls and ceiling, and hid the entrance to this Tomb of the Guardians. Sealing off all access both to them and to what they guarded. We knew that some murdering traitor was prowling in the vaults, though I did not yet suspect you, my son."

"You never did suspect me!" Floriano's ugly, spiteful laugh at his father. "I can still see your face, when that fat old fool of a colonel told you that I had accused you. *I!*" He laughed again, but suddenly the laughter stopped.

Yet Prince Mino's face looked as impassive as ever. "You were afraid then, as you are afraid now. But with less cause."

In those quiet words was something very frightening. Something that left the statue-filled room extremely silent, in some way very cold.

Prince Mino himself broke that silence. "Our reckoning nears, but I will keep my word. First you shall see what all these years you have dreamed of seeing. What Mania's priests—gold-greedy tricksters though you think them—gave their lives to guard."

"Where is it?" Once again, Floriano had forgotten all else. "Where is it?"

There was an altar; I had been so busy looking at all the works of marvelous craftsmanship that I had hardly noticed it until now. Prince Mino walked around it, stooped, and lifted two dully gleaming bronze caskets that he laid upon the smooth stone surface of its top.

With a cry like a hungry beast's Floriano sprang. My knees bumped hard against the altar stone as he sank to his, both hands clawing at the nearer casket.

"Stop!" His father's voice cut through that trance of greed. Floriano obeyed, his hands still curved like talons.

"If those chests held trash they would still be priceless." Was Prince Mino's grim contempt mixed with pain? "Yet to you—whom I still believe to have sprung from my own loins—they are worthless, save for their contents. Look at them; that at least you shall do! Look!"

I did look. Those caskets were works of art. Warriors, monsters, weird sphinxes crowned their exquisitely carved sides. The handle of one was formed by two tiny winged figures carrying a cauldron; that of its mate by a dead warrior borne between two living comrades, grief plain upon the miniature faces beneath their thumbnail-sized helmets. All the figures were perfect, even to the nails upon the toes of their tiny feet.

I don't think Floriano ever saw them. He just knelt there, panting in savage impatience. For so many years he had dreamed of this hour: of the golden discovery that would lift him above all slights, real or imagined, give him power and prestige—those ancient substitutes for self-respect—as well as splendor and luxury. Deep down inside himself, he must have believed that the glory of that sight would give him strength to sweep his father and all other obstacles from his path.

And his father stood there and kept him waiting.

The mad irony of it all suddenly struck me: an old man who was about to take two human lives hurt, even outraged by his son's disrespect for two pieces of carved metal; a young man who was about to die thinking of nothing but gold that he never would get a chance to spend. I could have laughed at both of them, although I was about to die too. Prince Mino might have been sentimental about his old servant, but he wasn't going to be sentimental about Floriano. Or me.

"Stand back, my son." At last Prince Mino moved.

With deft, loving fingers he opened one casket. Even more lovingly he lifted out the contents, carefully laying down roll after roll of dry-looking brown stuff.

Linen! Intricately figured linen, perhaps ages old.

A sobbing groan burst from Floriano, the kind of sound an animal might make in thwarted hunger. "The other! The other!"

Prince Mino opened the other casket, emptied it almost as carefully and gently. It held baked clay tablets, which seemed to bear the same queer figures as the linen, but there a few thin sheets of much tarnished metal. The old man looked down at them, and his face shone with ecstasy. There was a kind of glory on it.

"Treasure indeed, my son. Treasure beyond all the dreams that scholars have dreamed through the centuries."

Floriano howled like a wolf. Again he sprang at his father; again Prince Mino struck. Together Floriano and I crashed down upon the hard stones, and as I struggled to raise myself upon one arm, bruised and shaken, I heard him sobbing, moaning in utter misery: "Books! Books—only books!"

Bell-like again, Prince Mino's voice rang out above us. "The lost *Etruscan Discipline*, that Augustus once enshrined in Rome's holiest temple. He had only copies, that great emperor—copies written in the bastard alphabet inspired by the corrupting Greeks. I have the originals, written in characters that were ancient long before the Rasenna landed in Italy. Long before Knossos fell; maybe before Menes united the Two Lands and made Egypt a nation. Characters that inspired the hieroglyphs of the Maya, that great American people whose books fanatical Spanish savages destroyed even as Rome destroyed the Rasenna."

He paused, looking down at me. I believe he really thought I would be interested.

"Yes, your first, your only true North American civilization, signora—not a poor copy of Europe's so-called, tasteless, mechanized civilization, such as you have now—was inspired, like all other great cultures, by the Rasenna. Soon now I will know the history of that last migration—and of the first! I will know where Tyrrha stood, the first, the true Tyrrha, that 'High Place' from whose flame Egypt and Sumer and all the others lit their poor candles! For at last I have found the key! At last I can read the ancient, lost tongue of the Rasenna!"

The face of that last high priest who buried himself with his threatened temple and its treasures never can have looked more dedicated, more terrible, in its all-sacrificing exaltation. I thought, shivering, that now at last I knew how a madman looked.

CHAPTER X

As suddenly as it had come, the madness faded from his fierce old face. It became again the fine, high-bred mask.

"But I speak to children, creatures without understanding.... Your pardon, signora. Rise, my son." He stooped and helped me to my feet as Floriano stumbled to his. "Thanks to this young man's impetuosity, I fear that I have also caused you pain."

Floriano's face was still bleeding from the third blow, his eyes were dull and lusterless. He moved like an old man, the will to live, even his hate, gone out of him.

Silently we left that buried temple, Prince Mino moving as silently behind us. The way back up must have been as long as the way down had been, but I remember very little about it. Nothing except that every step, the time it took to take that step, seemed precious, something irrevocably lost. As of course it was. Every movement, every moment, is one less out of our allotted span of life. And the prince had kept his promise, shown us his treasure. There was nothing more for him to wait for.

Our time was bound to be very short indeed.

The vast cavern was gone forever, and so was the snake-like hissing of that steam-crowned abyss. We were out of that suffocating passage, back in the Tomb of the Priests. My lantern still stood there, lighting the great round chamber, even lessening the darkness of some of those niches that for ages had been beds of the dead.

"This way, signora. I know that you are tired, but one more sight I must ask you to see before you rest." The regret, the considerateness in the prince's voice made it almost gentle, but his face was still as cold and hard as the faces of the carven dead.

He led us towards the far side of the room, where the shadows were deepest. Objects began to loom up through them, took shape. One of the niches held a cot, camp chair, and table, all folded. In the next were a primus stove, a loaf of bread, and some cans and utensils.

"Comforts provided me by my good Mattia." The prince's voice was now as expressionless as his face.

I thought of all the luxury in the villa above. As an avenger, Floriano had not done badly. Yet, to do Prince Mino justice, I believe that if that mask hid grief, it was all for the old man who had tried to make him comfortable.

"Life in the cave might have been safer, had it not been for the odor. Even living here, I have considered a nightly walk in the open air above essential to my physical fitness. But for a while now, I must change both my quarters and my habits. My notes and papers I have already removed to the cavern. Death soon will be sole lord again in this ancient chamber." Why did he smile faintly, subtly, as he said that?

"You can't stay here at all without old Mattia to bring you food!" I grasped at a sudden hope. "I'm sure my husband will help you. Let me talk to him—"

"To that poor unconscious man, signora?" Again that cutting curl of his lip.

"I meant when he wakes up, of course! Do believe me—do help him! If I'd ever been in love with your son, I'd certainly be over it now."

"The love of women is a strange thing, signora. I dare not trust to your change of heart. One or two of the villagers knew me well of old. Through one or other of them, help will reach your husband, as I have promised, and future supplies will reach me, though neither can take the place of Mattia Rossi." He sighed. "Truly I expected you, my son; I have waited long for you. But you have added one more crime to the list for which you must be punished. That has altered my plans somewhat, even for you."

Floriano shivered and swayed; he must have been

near collapse. Blows, exertion, loss of blood, all must have taken their toll, magnificent animal though he was. I saw Prince Mino shoot him a quick glance. "You are faint, my son? You would like some brandy? And you, signora?"

We both shook our heads. I think we had both of us reached that point when fear itself becomes unbearable, when anything, even the blow itself, is better than waiting for it to fall....

"As you please. Now for that sight I promised you. I have not been lonely here. The bones of the old Tequna have been good company, but also I have those who once bore my name, members of my own house."

He swung his torch beam along the curving wall, towards the third berth left of that which held his furniture. Into a niche that had been undiluted blackness....

Part of me must have fainted then, though my body still stood upright.

Side by side they lay, their skulls still close together upon the rotted remnants of what once must have been a silken pillow. Two skeletons, still covered by a mass of bits and pieces of rotten silk. I saw them, and I saw something else—the heavy, rusty iron chain that still bound them together, stapled them to the wall behind what had been their heads. And though it was what I had expected to see, everything went black....

When I woke, I was lying on something softer than rock. Horrifyingly, I thought of that rotten silk. My eyes flashed open, I looked down, and saw that I was lying on Prince Mino's camp cot. Then I heard Prince Mino's voice.

"You should be happy now, my son. You are seeing what none ever has seen before, save the legitimate heir of the Carenni. As my father showed it to me, I show it to you."

Floriano made some sort of strangled noise; he evidently did not appreciate the honor. His father went on, "He was taken by surprise, our ancestor. Mad with grief and fury, he plunged his sword into the boy when he found those two lying in their guilt. She in whose arms that shamer of his house lay, she whose crime was the lesser because no Carenni blood flowed in her veins, she paid the greater penalty. That was no true *bella vendetta.* Both lovers should have lain here living, have been left alone in this age-old silence to learn which first forgot love and turned to tear the other—!"

Floriano's voice cut across his, shrill as a woman's. "What are you talking about? What has this evil old madness to do with us?"

Prince Mino's quiet voice was quelling. "You will do your house this one service, Floriano. You will undergo the penalty that that other young traitor of our blood should have paid. Here, my son, in the next niche, you shall lie. With your bedfellow."

The handcuffs! They were to bind Floriano and me together forever, as the chain still bound those two skeletons: the chain that had been put upon them when both still had young, lovely flesh. When the girl had been alive—I knew then that, deep down, I had feared this all along. With all my own doomed flesh.

For a minute I must have been unconscious again. Floriano's shriek roused me: a hideous, inhuman howl that seemed as if it would bring down the roof. Then, after a moment's hush, he began sobbing, pleading. The tone made his meaning clear, although Prince Mino was no longer making him speak English. No doubt because he thought me still unconscious, me, the providentially supplied pawn he could use in his son's punishment. But why didn't Floriano's voice sound nearer? He must be standing night at my side.

I opened my eyes, looked down at my wrist. No handcuff was there. I looked again, I stared, but both my wrists were free, blessedly free. When I had fallen and the camp cot had been put up—oh, that horrible, considerate courtesy of Prince Mino's!—the cuffs must have been in the way. The prince had freed me.

Could I possibly get away now while he was enjoying his son's piteous outburst? At least I must try. My shoes would make a noise on the stone floor. Cautiously I sat up, took them off. Holding them in one hand, I swung myself carefully, very carefully, to the floor. But the cot creaked. My heart stood still. Neither man moved, however. Floriano's pitiful pleading still went on, and apparently his father had ears for nothing else.

I tiptoed towards the great doorway. At every step I

expected to hear Prince Mino's voice. I wanted to run, to look back over my shoulder, but if I did either, here among all these dancing shadows, I might stumble and really make a noise.

I was through the doorway, outside in that short passage that I think the Greeks would have called a *dromos*. I still couldn't run; it was quite dark here.

"NO!" Back inside the tomb, Floriano's agonized cry rose to a shriek. *"No!"*

"Disobey me, and you will suffer for that disobedience. And still lie there. Would you make your pain greater than even I choose to make it? Lie down."

The wail that followed was like nothing else that I have ever heard, something that I wish I did not have to remember. Another came, and another, and I did run—as if devils were behind me, as indeed they were. The black silence of the labyrinth received me, sweet as welcoming arms. I ran until I bumped into a wall and knocked myself down. I put on my shoes, then scrambled up and ran on, hands outstretched before me, as I blindly made turn after turn. Until some unevenness in the stones of the floor tripped me, and I fell again.

That time I lay there, too spent to rise. Expecting every instant to have Prince Mino's flashlight blaze in my eyes, to hear his cold voice. But I saw nothing, heard nothing but my own breathing. Nothing else broke that terrible, stony silence. Dead silence, that was like part of the stone itself: a foretaste of death.

I realized the truth then. *I'm lost. I never can find my way out of this maze. Unless somebody comes I'll die here, alone in the dark.*

But nobody could come except Prince Mino, and then I would still die in the dark, but chained to Floriano. Better, far better, to die alone.

I don't know what finally made me understand; somehow knowledge came to me out of the silence and the blackness that were as calm as himself. Prince Mino was not coming. My flight had been exactly what he wanted. Deliberately he had chosen words to frighten me, make me run away. My body, found here with no marks of violence on it, might well keep searchers from going deeper into the vaults, unearthing him. He had even spared himself the physical ugliness of having to kill someone he did not hate. Clever, clever Prince Mino!

I couldn't imagine what he really had done to Floriano; I didn't want to know. But he was a man of honor; he had promised to help Richard, and he would. As for myself—well, I was too tired to care. I pillowed my head on one arm, and relaxed. There was a kind of relief in giving up, in not fighting any more....

· · · · · ·

"Bar-bara! Bar-ba-ra!" From far away a voice was calling me. Calling me back from the quiet un-dark place, the good place, where I had found refuge, back into a darkness that was not good.... As I came back into my body, I heard it more clearly.

"Bar-ba-ra! Barb!"

Richard's voice! Had he died, all alone in that lovely, sinister room far above? Died and then come back, down into this underworld, to find me?

"Barbs!" This time his voice sounded farther away. Why should it, if he were dead?

I jumped to my feet, called out with all the strength left in me: "Richard! Richard!"

His voice leapt across the distance and the darkness, eager, exultant: "Barby! Where are you?"

He was there, he was real!

I don't remember much about those next few minutes, that blind, anxious stumbling and running, as we groped towards each other's voices. When a flashlight blazed in my eyes, I jerked back, remembering Prince Mino. But Richard's voice came from behind it, "Barb!" And then we were in each other's arms, kissing hungrily, clumsily. Floriano would have sneered at our technique, but to us it was good, good. He said huskily, "Barb, honey. Barb...."

I said, "You woke up, Richard. You woke up!"

He said grimly, "I woke up a good while ago, Barby. While that fellow Floriano was pounding on the door and cursing you."

"Then—when I ran away?" It took me a minute to remember; everything that had happened before Prince

Mino came seemed so long ago. "But when he brought me back, you never stirred—"

"I was in no shape to take him on. I'm still a bit wobbly."

"Oh, I should have thought! Let's sit down."

We did, and I knew that he was glad of the wall to lean against. He turned off the flashlight, saying that we must save the battery, and I said, thinking back, "So that's where that last cup of coffee went. I thought there ought to be one more in the pot."

"That cup saved my life. Or I felt as if it did. When I'd rested a little while, I made another pot, and drank all of that. I had some toast too. You and your would-be boyfriend were gone quite a while. Long enough to make me sweat blood."

"And when you did come, you just lay there—and listened?" My cheeks burned.

"Honey, the best moment of my life was when I heard your voice and knew you were all right." His own voice, that had been very serious, suddenly broke into a laugh. "If he'd known you half as well as I do, you couldn't have fooled for a minute. If you'd ever pulled that damn fool giggle on me you'd still be safe in America, a single woman."

"What would you have done if—?"

"I'd have cracked him over the head with this flashlight. I kept it in my hand, under the covers, just in case. Even if I wasn't at my best, surprise would have been on my side, that time."

"That time?" I didn't understand.

"You didn't think I was fool enough to crack up my car on the way into the garage, did you?" He sounded insulted.

"You mean—Floriano—?"

"I'd just started the car when I saw him in the rear-view mirror. I let out a gasp, and that was my mistake. He was prepared for emergencies; he had a wrench in his hand, and he hit me over the head. He must have jumped clear as the car crashed. I don't know how on Earth I got out."

"I tried to help you." I began to shiver again, and he held me closer, said quietly, "Tell me about it."

I did, ending, "He must have followed me to the car, and have hidden in the trunk, Richard—there in Volterra. He was the escaped prisoner the police were looking for; I figured that part out. But I never thought of his having hurt you—tried to kill you—" The shivering started again, but when he kissed me it stopped.

"Thanks. You certainly saved my life. But you've had some mighty narrow squeaks yourself. When you and dear Floriano left our rooms, I sweated a good deal more blood. I couldn't move fast enough to spring on him, and when I followed you it seemed to be at a snail's pace. Then when I saw Prince Mino, I thought that crack in my head must be a lot worse than I'd figured."

"Why? You didn't know him."

"I did. I'd seen photographs, and Dr. Pulcinelli had

told me he was dead. For a while I must have been just plain groggy; then when I saw the three of you going downstairs—"

"You couldn't have followed us all this way!"

"No. I'm ashamed to say I blacked out at the head of the cellar stairs. When I came to, I realized I'd have no chance to find you in all this maze down here; I couldn't see Prince Mino stopping in the wine cellar. So I just sat there with my trusty flashlight in my hand, and waited for whoever should come up."

"Then how did you get here?"

"Prince Mino brought me. I'm glad I was feeling a little too dopey to cosh him when he came up."

"You—met—Prince Mino?"

"Yes. The old fellow was very decent. He gave me some brandy from his flask, and I told him I'd been hurt in an accident, and thought you must have gone down to the wine cellar to find something reviving, but that you'd been gone so long I was getting worried."

"Do you think he believed you?"

"I have no idea. He said the telephone was out of order, and that since he'd sent old Mattia on an errand, he'd have to fix it himself; that once he'd phoned for help, he'd go down to look for you. But I said that if he started for the telephone, I'd start after you by myself. In the end we came down here together."

"You went—with him?" I felt cold with fear, although he was safe here beside me. I didn't think until later what fear he must have felt for me during that long, awful time of waiting. Of all the misery and anxiety and physical exertion that his light words masked.

That must have been a strange journey that the two men made into the depths. Prince Mino professed great surprise that Richard had known nothing of his "projected visit" to the villa. "But our good friend Professor Harris did not expect me so soon; my doctors have been most cautious. My good Mattia was truly overjoyed at sight of me."

"He kept leading me farther and farther down. Always saying that if you hadn't gone this way, you must have gone that way. Until I knew that actually we were playing the spider and the fly. I kept my feet partly because of the brandy—he gave me a couple more swigs—but mostly because I knew I had to.

"We finally came to a pair of enormous stone doors, and I decided that I'd gone far enough; whatever was behind those doors, it was probably the spider's parlor. I sat down—flopped down, rather; said I had to. He believed that; I'd already had to rest several times. He even seemed pleased, said he'd go in and see if the room was just as he had left it; it had been the scene of some of his most important discoveries. He did go in; he actually shut the doors behind him. I wondered why."

I didn't. He had been afraid that Floriano's cries might still be heard from within. I felt sick.

"I took a chance." Richard was still speaking. "I followed him and wedged those doors shut with my clasp knife. He can't open them. He tried. I saw those immense stone doors move—just a little—but there was no sound. I called to him. I put my mouth to a tiny crack there in one place between the doors; I told him I'd seen you with him, and with another, younger man who'd already roughed you up and dragged you back when you'd tried to go for help. I said I had a gun and I'd let him out if he brought you with him. But he never made a sound. Not one sound."

He stopped. I knew that once again he was feeling that silence, the awful chill of it. I could feel it too.

He said slowly, "I was worried, about as worried as a man can be. You might just possibly have been in there. Barbara—" His arms tightened around me. For a little we didn't say anything. Then he said matter-of-factly, "We'd better be getting out of here. Back upstairs."

I said in fresh panic, "But how will we ever find our way out of here?" and Richard chuckled in answer, waved a bit of white muslin under my nose. "We owe the Harrises for a sheet. When I followed you and Floriano, I pulled this off the bed and carried it along. I thought that if I could knock him, we might tear it up and tie him up with it. But when I came down here I cut it up for markers instead."

I stared, then understood. "You mean you dropped a little piece every time you went around a turn? Like the children in the fairy tale, only they used pebbles. Oh, Richard, you're wonderful!"

"Fairly so, but I can't claim originality. I remembered the fairy tale. So did Prince Mino. When he first saw me cut out a bit and drop it, he explained that since he was with me that was quite unnecessary. But I was a sick man, so he decided to humor my cowardly nerves." Now Richard's smile was dry.

Whatever he was doing, Prince Mino was no longer smiling. The trapper was trapped, shut up in his own lair. He too must be feeling like a cornered beast now. It is always terrible to think of pride broken; though he had been wrong and cruel and wicked, I felt sorry for him. But only for a moment. Then I slipped my arm through Richard's; I knew that he was going to need all the support I could give him.

They never failed us, those bits of white muslin. Not one turn had Richard missed, half-fainting though he must have been. We made many stops, some of them short, some seemingly long, but finally we made it.

Richard was reeling, wheezing with exhaustion, when at last we reached the ground floor of the villa. He collapsed onto the first sofa we came to, a lovely ornate thing, and I covered him up with a throw rug, then dropped down myself. The floor here was stone too, but the rich, thick rug on it felt like heaven after the bare rock I had been getting used to. That is the last thing I remember....

A tremendous crash woke me. I jumped up, then sank back, afraid. The whole world seemed to be rocking beneath me. The floor shook; from below came more crashes, muffled now, deep, horrible noises as if some titanic monster were grinding up stone walls in his teeth.

"Richard, what is it?" I caught his hand. He was sitting up on the sofa now.

"An earth tremor, Barbs. They have them in this country, you know. It'll be over in a minute."

I thought of the depths below. "Richard, what is happening—down there?"

He said very gently, "It's already happened, honey. And I think it's better this way. Now Prince Mino never will have to go to either of those grim-looking places in Volterra."

For the first time I remembered those stored explosives that had worried Roger Carstairs, remembered and understood. Prince Mino had thought as Richard thought. As long ago, when Sulla's men drew near, the high priest of Mania must have thought....

The subterranean shaking and crashing had ceased. Light streamed in through the windows; the golden morning lay quiet around us. The morning of a new day.

CHAPTER XI

Those ponderous stone doors that once led to the Tomb of the High Priests still stand, though split and riven, but the chamber behind them must be a solid mass of fallen rock. When the *carabinieri* came, they shook their heads. "To dig out a trace of those two men would take a fortune, signore. Nor could we identify them then. There would be no faces, no bodies even. Not a bone that was not splintered."

So the Tomb of the Guardians no longer exists. Neither can that weird passage that wound down from it; that secret way that for thousands of years no man had ever trod never will be trodden by any man again. Does the terrible shape of Mania herself still stand, down there in those abysmal depths? Richard thinks that possibly—just possibly—it may, that that roof that was not reared by the hands of man may have withstood the shock of the cataclysm.

"But I'll never get down there to see, Barby." He sighed; he will always envy me my sight of the temple. "Nowadays archaeologists can't get hold of the kind of money it would take to dig that place out again. Not when the chances of its survival are so slim, and the evidence so vague. You are the only witness, and you've had no archaeological training."

"If you had let me tell the police who Prince Mino really was, Richard—not just let them think he was some unknown criminal associate of Floriano's who quarreled with him—"

"We can't prove his identity, and if we could we'd only make trouble for the doctor he blackmailed into letting him go." Richard added gently, "He never was too sane, honey. And he'd lived too far underground too long. That yarn about Etruscan manuscripts written in something like Maya characters—"

"I'd think being suspected of Roger's murder would hurt his memory more. But you have a point about the doctor."

"Also Prince Mino can't be cleared of murder. He died the murderer of his own son."

"Yes, he did do that. And I wish he'd let Floriano be hanged. Whenever I think of the way whatever he did do sounded—" I shuddered, remembering those wails.

Richard said soberly, "I think I know what happened. But do you really want to hear?"

"Knowing's always better than imagining things."

"You and Floriano both seem to have thought that

the Prince carried Mattia Rossi's body down to the abyss. But to have taken it down that narrow passage-way you describe would have been very hard for one old man. Hard on both him and it. My guess is that he put it in a sarcophagus in the Tomb of the Guardians. And that when you fainted he made Floriano open that sarcophagus. That would explain that first shriek you heard."

I shuddered again, at the picture those words evoked. "But those later wails? They were awful!"

Richard said very quietly, "In that famous passage of Virgil's, the man whom the Etruscan king leaves to die is bound to another man's body. Not to a woman."

Well, I hope Prince Mino can rest. Richard later found confirmation of his theory, something that the *carabinieri* had missed. Something that must have been pushed out from under those stone doors carefully, delicately, with some very fine thin instrument like a steel yardstick. Only a trained searcher like Richard ever could have fished it out of all the debris that lies heaped before the Tomb of the Guardians. But as Richard says, "It had to be there. He couldn't have gone without a word. He wasn't the type."

It was a neatly folded sheet of paper addressed to

Richard Keyes, Esq.

in a bold, precise, yet delicate hand. Unfolded, it read:

"My dear signore:

"I trust that by now you have found your lovely lady, and that soon neither of you will be the worse for your adventures. Permit me to offer you both my profound regrets for any inconvenience caused you by me or mine. I am only too well aware that our hospitality has not done credit to the Villa Carenni.

"Your story of the signora's flight and of my son's angry pursuit shows me that I did her a grave injustice, for which I most humbly beg her pardon; had I known the truth, she would have been spared certain sights and sounds which, I fear, caused her distress. Still, it is not altogether amiss for a young and beautiful woman occasionally to see something of how justice is done.

"You yourself, signore, I congratulate on the cleverness with which you outwitted me. Few men have done that, and no other with impunity. But I pardon you; you could not have been expected to understand the honor of the Carenni.

"You never had any cause to fear me; from the moment we met, I knew what I must do. Had I been fated once more to come out of this tomb chamber where so many of my possessions are still stored, we would

have drunk together again and I would have
drugged you, then have sought out your lady
and conveyed you both to a place of safety.
For one error I could not have permitted—
any presumptuous meddling with my son's
just sentence—and I was in no good position
to resist any such sentimental folly. I fired my
last bullet into that unfortunate young man
when I found him with the Signora Keyes."

I gasped. "Then he really was helpless! All the time.
Floriano and I were scared to death of an old man with
an empty gun!"

"The prince would have made a fine poker player,"
Richard said dryly. He read on:

"In what I must do now I shall miss the
help of my faithful Mattia, but it does not
greatly matter. An explosion here will harm
no real Etruscan antiquities, the tomb being
of so late a date. It will destroy the bones of
those who outraged my ancestor's honor,
but there are no more young Carenni to be
shown them.

"My one regret is that I must hasten my
son's release from his sufferings, but perhaps
they will not be greatly lessened. For some
time now I have heard no sound from him,
and though he does not deserve the mercy

of unconsciousness, I must confess that I am somewhat glad of quiet.

"He lies there now with his head beside Mattia's half-crushed, bloodstained gray head, and one of them makes no more sound than the other. Yet he made a great fuss when first he learned what his punishment was to be. I said, 'When you were a child, he did you many kindnesses, this old man you have butchered. Now while your sight lasts, you shall behold your handiwork.' I even taped his eyes so that he could not close them; that is one refinement that I think the old Rasenna did not know. And for a while the results were all that could be desired, yet now he lies as if he saw nothing. If I had more time I would try to rouse him....

"To some extent he has bested me. I see now that I never could have been the man to give my work to the world. In you I bequeath that task to a man of courage, integrity, and some scholarship. You will find my papers carefully arranged—"

All the rest was technical, the advice and instructions of one archaeologist to another. I saw Richard's face when he put the paper down and I said, perhaps awkwardly, "I'm sorry. I know that work would have meant a lot to you."

He grimaced. "Well, I'll never know exactly what I've missed. But I am sorry for the prince. He was no vandal; he'd never knowingly have risked destroying that temple or its treasures."

No, you were no vandal, Prince Mino. You never would have done intentional harm to precious old stone, only to sensitive, living flesh.

I said, "But that first explosion didn't go wrong. The one they staged just after Roger's death. I wonder what was the matter this time."

"Mattia Rossi was there then. He may have understood explosives better than Prince Mino. Also this time the pillar was weaker; that repair job never should have been tackled by two old men."

"And I suppose Prince Mino was too much of a megalomaniac ever to believe that anything he undertook could go wrong."

"He had to admit one failure, Barby. About the worst kind that a man can make. His own son destroyed him."

"He destroyed his son!" I felt a sudden flash of anger. "It wasn't all Floriano's fault. His father had no right to judge him; he'd helped to make him what he was."

"You always were a bit soft on that young devil, weren't you, Barby?" Richard's smile was quizzical.

I winced, felt my cheeks burn. "You've no idea what it was like, Richard, with you lying there as if you were dead. When Floriano came, he wasn't just beautiful—

he was the only warm, friendly thing in the world. I know I should just have been angry when he tried to make love to me, but—"

"You weren't?" Richard looked amused. "We're all human, honey, and some reactions are automatic, as inevitable as winds and tides. Since Floriano only tried to make love, I've got no kick coming. You didn't go overboard."

"No, I didn't. But I've felt like a fool ever since. And when Prince Mino was despising me, I felt like something a whole lot worse. I couldn't fight back."

"Forget him. Forget both of them. Come here." He grinned and held out his arms, and I came. We were happy. We never again have spoken of that part of what happened; Richard is not the man to rub things in. And now that we have lived together longer, loved each other longer, I understand much that I could not understand then. But I am still puzzled whenever I think of those two men that he told me to forget.

What kills it? The ability to love, to learn? Prince Mino once loved his wife; Floriano loved his mother; and in the capacity to love one thing, there must be the seed of the power to love all things. Yet Floriano, for all his magnificent maleness, was not a whole man. He and his father were alike, for all their unlikeness. What ate out their humanity—the capacity to feel pity, remorse, to share the joy and pain of other people? Yet those who feel either better or worse than their fellow humans always seem to end by being a little less than human.

I never loved Floriano, but I am glad that no pitiful travesty of his beauty still lies bound there in the depths. Glad, too, that those other poor bones, with the fetters that imprisoned them so long, have been crushed to powder by all those tons of rock, released at last. Somewhere I once read of an Eastern belief that the sense of guilt, justified or not, can bind a soul to Earth. If those poor young lovers were finally terrified into believing themselves as sinful as their murderer believed them, then their chains must have bound to that grim bed through all those centuries, in the dark.... But that is only a crazy fancy, surely. It could come only to one who also once had been judged by a Carenni.

Well, there are no more Carenni. All that summer, our first together, the villa was ours, Richard's and mine. He offered to take me away, and I was tempted. I thought of Eos, her great wings all white loveliness in the clean gold light of morning, and then turning to black terror in the dusk. But then I thought of Richard himself.

"There is still plenty of work you can do here, isn't there, Rick? Plenty of tombs that weren't hurt?"

He hesitated; I saw the longing in his face. "Yes. But this place is so full of endings, I don't believe it's the right one for a beginning."

"Yes, it is. Remember what you said the day we came here, Richard? That all old houses have seen both ugliness and beauty? I think this one's been cheated. Let's stay and give it a little of what it deserves."

So we stayed. Sometimes at first I used to wake in the night (Richard never knew that), hearing, not the explosion, but that terrible utter quiet in which Prince Mino must have sat, writing his last letter. Seeing the everlasting darkness of the tomb chamber pressing in upon him, closer and closer, until even the lamplight could not keep it back.... But always in the mornings, when I woke again beside Richard, I would know that I was glad. Glad to be there loving in the midst of all that loveliness. It is right that beauty should be rightly used.

Once Prince Mino said to Floriano, "As a child you brought laughter between these old walls that have known too little laughter." Maybe we have lessened even his darkness a little, lessening theirs. Between those walls our first child was conceived, Richard's son and mine. Soon he will be fathering his own children; all that terror was long ago.

I have done enough thinking, enough remembering. It is still my time to live.

AUTHOR'S NOTE

In one of the many non-fiction books written about the "Mysterious Etruscans," I found mention of a villa on top of a cliff into which ancient tombs had been built. Hence this book, which is fiction.

The goddess Mania is, if anything, even more mysterious than her own Etruscans. But we do know that human sacrifice was offered to her, and that Mantua, Dante's birthplace, was named for her consort Mantus, Lord of the Underworld. Underground temples did exist, and ancient writers, notably Pausanias, tell of the queer customs of chthonian sanctuaries, such as their being opened only once a year, entered only by dream-summoned worshippers, etc. And where could such weird rites have been more at home than among the Etruscans?

"The Island of Refuge" is a genuine tradition. For Prince Mino's theories, I take no responsibility, but some scholars have connected the Etruscans with both Atlantis and the American Indians. Hardly anybody agrees with them, but it would be nice to have some explanation for the peculiar fact that the Maya calendar dates back to a time thousands of years before any Maya cities were built.

—Evangeline Walton

AFTERWORD

At the time of her death in 1996 at age eighty-eight, Evangeline Walton's papers were found in great disorder. Those who have worked on the sorting and organizing of the archive—Walton's literary heir, Debra L. Hammond; her mother, Louise Hammond; and I—have been delighted by the various finds we have made, including unpublished short stories, plays, and novels. These manuscripts date from the 1920s through the early 1990s. Although Walton frequently had difficult relations with publishers, and although she was often diffident about offering her work for publication, she published seven novels during her lifetime.

According to a letter Walton wrote in 1974, *She Walks in Darkness* (originally titled *She Who Goes Winged*) was written in the 1960s, subsequent to some of her worst experiences with a publisher. In 1956, Thomas

Bouregy of the New York firm Bouregy & Curl had severely edited her novel of the conflict between the Norsemen and the English in the early eleventh century, *Dark Runs the Road*, cutting pages and sections while rewriting it, shortening it, and retitling it *The Cross and the Sword*—all of which was done against the author's wishes. The contract Walton had signed required that she offer Bouregy & Curl her next completed novel, and after the rude treatment she had received from Bouregy personally, she simply held onto this next completed manuscript and didn't offer it anywhere.

Then, in 1970, her first published novel, *The Virgin and the Swine* (1936), based on the Fourth Branch of the Mabinogion, was rediscovered and republished as *The Island of the Mighty* in the Ballantine Adult Fantasy series. Betty Ballantine and Lin Carter (the editorial consultant for the series) were happy to learn that Walton had existing versions of other branches of the Mabinogion, and Walton felt free to publish them with Ballantine because they had originally been written long before her contract with Bouregy. These three books include *The Children of Llyr* (1971), *The Song of Rhiannon* (1972), and *Prince of Annwn* (1974).

After submitting the final manuscript of *Prince of Annwn*, Walton turned her attention back to *She Walks in Darkness*, and with the assistance of a lawyer, she cleared away her contractual obligation to Bouregy. In the meantime, Ballantine Books had been sold and the Adult Fantasy series closed down. Walton submitted the manuscript to her new literary agent, who told her that the market for Gothic had dried up, so Walton stored the manuscript in her files and returned to her trilogy of novels about Theseus, which she had first written in the mid-1940s and rewritten in the mid-1950s but set aside when Mary Renault's *The King Must Die* became a bestseller in 1958. Walton managed to rewrite and publish the first Theseus novel, *The Sword Is Forged*, in 1983, and she worked on revising the two subsequent novels, but they remained unpublished at her death.

In an interview in September 1985, Walton noted: "I had a Gothic novel ready just when the Gothic craze expired, and I'd like to get that out someday. And there's a children's story I once wrote for a young cousin, *The Forest That Would Not Be Cut Down*. That's the only title that expresses it, and yet it's too long to be used, I'm afraid. This forest has a magical ability to protect itself which, unfortunately, real forests lack."

It is good that *She Walks in Darkness* is finally seeing publication, and we hope that further manuscripts from her archive may see print in the future.

—Douglas A. Anderson